THERE ARE NO ELDERS

THERE ARE NO ELDERS

AUSTIN CLARKE

Exile Editions

Publishers of
Fiction, Poetry, Essays, Drama, and Art
2007

Library and Archives Canada Cataloguing in Publication

Clarke, Austin, 1934-
    There are no elders / Austin Clarke ; introduction by Leon Rooke.

(Exile classics ; no. 5)

Originally published 1993.

ISBN 978-1-55096-092-1

    I. Title. II. Series.

PS8505.L38T46 2007   C813'.54   C2007-901994-3

Design and Composition by Homunculus ReproSet
Cover Painting by Joe Morse
Typeset in Garamond at the Moons of Jupiter Studios
Printed in Canada by Gauvin Imprimerie

The publisher would like to acknowledge the financial assistance of
The Canada Council for the Arts, and the Ontario Arts Council–which is
an agency of the Government of Ontario.

 Conseil des Arts   Canada Council
du Canada   for the Arts

 ONTARIO ARTS COUNCIL
CONSEIL DES ARTS DE L'ONTARIO

Published in Canada in 2007 by Exile Editions Ltd.
144483 Southgate Road 14
General Delivery
Holstein, Ontario, N0G 2A0
info@exileeditions.com
www.ExileEditions.com

Canadian Sales Distribution: U.S. Sales Distribution:
McArthur & Company   Independent Publishers Group
c/o Harper Collins   814 North Franklin Street
1995 Markham Road   Chicago, IL 60610
Toronto, ON M1B 5M8   www.ipgbook.com
toll free: 1 800 387 0117   toll free: 1 800 888 4741

CONTENTS

INTRODUCTION

One of the fascinating things about this fine collection of stories by Austin Clarke — no, better make that *superb*, and make it a *cycle* too, for these stories (each one lovely) work together like a dream . . . one of the things I most relish, anyway, is the extraordinary presence in the book of the author himself. Frequently he strolls the page in luminous dignity, honey in motion, your friendly correspondent wearing no disguise whatsoever. More often he goes undercover — jabbing, feinting, poking and prying, orbiting his way through a story's hidden warrens with the finesse of the original Artful Dodger. In few works of fiction is an author so reliably and engagingly present. The way he's *there* creates a reader/writer bonding that is rare in its intimacy and its warmth; this deepens our response to what is painful here and what is joyful, adds another layer to it all, takes nothing whatever away (for that's what these stories *are:* the writer in motion, lapping up his very particular world, looping his way through it). And it provides great fun, I would think, whether one knows Austin or comes upon him here as a stranger might.[1]

These are Toronto stories, and they are stories of the West Indies. In the last story in the book, for example, we have Toronto in the now (our man trudging through the snow, riding his train) and Barbados back then (our boy sitting on the sand, staring at a ship or at a "black, patched tube," a lifesaver that is drifting out to sea). The book's last sentence — spoken by an old, old friend not seen in fifty years, once the boy he sat with on that beach, now come upon by dazzling chance on Yonge

---

[1] For a fine portrait of the visible Clarke the reader may look up "Austin Clarke: Riding the Trane" in Barry Callaghan's *Raise You Ten* (McArthur & Company, 2006, pp. 263-69).

Street, another successful island man who's apt like him to be awash in memory and martinis – is "Goddamn! And you still don't know how to swim!" But swim he does, like a blasted master, Austin Clarke, between these worlds and within each one of them.

They are stories partly about racism:

"Nevermindthat!"
"Why never mind that?"
"Nevermindthat!"

The two women speaking here to the racism that riddles their lives (how much to the fore should this plague be in this instant, must it be always?) are two of a five-member group of island women waiting their turn under the iron at Christophe's Salon, best in the city for "fixing" black women's hair. They are here because this is where they have always come. So "nevermind" too the hard plastic chairs in this grungy salon, and "nevermind" their foreign cars parked below or their fine clothes or the fancy lunch they just had at the Four Seasons Hotel with two martinis each. They like it here. They are together, knitting up, weaving between, their various personal West Indian and Toronto stories and their responses to the drama that is suddenly happening at Christophe's Salon right now.

The story is "If the Bough Breaks," the first one in the book, and the five talking women constitute a kind of Greek Chorus, providing both overture and running commentary, a site of critique for all that Austin Clarke is doing in his book. They had to be women and mothers. In the other stories there is generally the figure of a man who is in some way our author, so this first story is and is not a different kind of story: the matrix from which all the others are born. It is important for the author that these are middle-class women whose lives contain much pleasure and that their experience of racism is nonetheless deeply engrained, a daily sorrow and source of rage. It's also no accident that the last story in the book, the one about those old-time friends who meet by chance on Yonge Street, is decidedly *male* and that it's called "The Cradle Will Fall." (Thus, the first and last stories work together as gendered "bookends" for the collection.)

All women know it, really all of us people know it: if the bough breaks, the cradle will fall. And the women on whom their sons and daughters depend cannot always protect them from the harsh and bitter wind. Sometime or many times along the way – early on, or in the middle, or at the end of a normal lifespan – that bough will break, and will be patched up one more time or not. In the last story, about the joy of "these two old black men . . . embracing and laughing and pummeling each other on their thick black cashmere winter coats," about their boyhood and their alcoholic beverages of choice and their sorrows and satisfactions and all the women along the way, it is clear that the cradle, though still rocking, will fall soon for good.

Because they have somehow become old. It's harder now to move through ice and snow, and there has been an increase in the habit of "dozing off." The conch shell that was blown when they were boys on the sand and an uncle was drowned will sometime soon be raised to someone's lips again to sound forth their deaths. But the author-figure who is "walking in the snow" is at the same time a boy "sitting on the sand" with his friend; and his same-but-different friend with an identical posh coat, still sitting in the bar even though it's closed, says this for both of them as the story nears its end:

"We leave the cradle, man, and our mothers feed
us Cream of Wheat to make us men and we have

different paths, and we go here and we go there, have women, wives, girlfriends, but we never leave the place we're born. We never grow up, really."

This passage echoes the lines from poet Derek Walcott that Austin Clarke quotes before *There Are No Elders* begins, and makes a claim that is both general and particularly West Indian. That children generally – and maybe sons most particularly – don't ever grow up, not really, is a thing their mothers know.

But in the first story it's daughters that the five women – in *their* posh clothes, after *their* martinis – are most worried about. Outside the salon, sirens scream, and the cop cars arrive; the women lean out of the salon windows to see a young white girl being led away. They'd been sure it would be a young black man, or maybe a young black woman, but black for sure – even though, they say, they raise their own children better than those blasted white people do. Cops are racist. But that's not all of it. Will they rape her in the car? She's just a *child*, some mother's child, and how much does it matter to their level of concern that this somebody's daughter is coloured white? They're worrying about their daughters too. And if the cops aren't the ones who've abused the young white girl who later comes into the salon, battered and bleeding, who is the niece of the man in the convenience store below, if it's someone closer like an uncle, shouldn't they maybe call the cops? They are drawn together "in their fear and their horror at the spectacle" (as Greek tragedy demands), and they ponder what they know:

> ...they went back over all those times, when their own children had been left with uncles and brothers-in-law, with close friends of their families, with

their own husbands, fathers of their children, and they dared not travel back with too much memory and clarity and honesty. There was blood on her leg.... They knew it could be one thing only. One cause. One kind of violence.

Working together, they try to soothe this poor female child, to patch her up, to cleanse her as best they can. One of them then poses a question that this book needs to ask: "Why is it always this way with women? And for women?"

So the stories of *There Are No Elders* are often concerned with race (roots and racism) and often too with sexuality and gender (sexual pleasure and fear and violence, and the pain and the distance between men and women). One of the strongest stories in the collection is the second one, titled "Ship, Sail! Sail Fast!" – words from childhood that are revisited in the final story. This story opens in a small, slow lakeside town outside Toronto and mostly spins out from the train journey that the author-figure, who "felt like a man escaping custody," takes to get back to "the big city." What he's escaping is a brief affair with a woman who has irritated him mightily by being a "woman who loved kissing the dog, and kissing him afterwards with the same lips," and by having "a plastic cover on the toilet bowl that he had to sit sideways on" as well as a "shower which beat against the sides of its tin enclosure" – all of it too small for him, another disappointment with womankind. But the paltriness of his irritation is as apparent to the reader as the deadly accuracy of its depiction; the eye of judgment in the story fixes *him*, and "Ship, Sail! Sail Fast!" is not a story in which the male of our species is triumphant.

From the taxi on his way to the train, the man sees a huge ship motionless – stalled – on the lake. It is an image that takes him back to the sea of his childhood. The story moves through images, between the parallel, moving planes of the train and the landscape it passes through, moves with breathtaking skill between memories of the woman he has just left and his West Indian youth. The sight of cornfields takes him to the young island girl who was "his only rudder, leading him into the valley of information and learning," and whose rebuke of a modest sexual advance stopped him in his tracks for fifteen years; it was that long "before he had the strength to raise his hand from his side to touch a woman on her waist." And that vulnerability, that fear of the power of rejection, even if it's hard to believe as many as *fifteen* years, changes how we place him in the story of the sexes.

But the most stunning thing – the extended, fast-beating heart of the story – is how the cornfields call into his imagination the time of slavery and the underground railroad. The figure of a woman appears, emerging "from the deep green patch of corn to hail the train," and the author-figure (he is not identified as a writer) knows instantly that her name is Jane. She is walking beside Jim, "her disappointment, her hindrance from catching the train that would have brought her sooner to glory and the freedom she was seeking." The author-figure can see clearly as well "the man's disappointment. And the man's shame. For the man knew he was a man, even in the circumscribed circumstance of his life and of his woman's life. But he had no power to behave as a man." They exist in different time periods and places, Jim and Jane, these figures given flesh and story by a writer's racing imagination; and we have before our astonished eyes a passionate history of how life has gone and how it goes for many black men and black women. (For example: when Jim cannot bear any longer the master's whip – there is "no unmarked area the size of a postage stamp" on his body – he "pushed her forward, to take her rightful place of leadership, and she took and endured the sting of justice.")

"In an Elevator" is a story (like many others here) with a rapidly zig-zagging point of view and overlapping voices. It is again a piece in which we are conscious of the writer's construction of what might be going on in the minds of unknown people, how observed scraps of the external world can generate character and theme and story. The principal story concerns a white woman who finds herself going down on an elevator with a young black man; she imagines that she is in sexual danger, and he sees her imagining this. The author-figure here appears only very briefly in the course of another elevator ride, this one going up, that the woman had taken a few days earlier. He is a black man on his way to an interview; he is well-dressed, pleasant, but she doesn't return his smile or speak. She is uncomfortable in his presence, and later that afternoon "she'd accused herself for having *those* feelings"; and she'd recalled a girl from Barbados she'd known at school and "that other one from the Bahamas who thought she was the cat's meow better than any of us with her father the prime minister." (She'd got back at that uppity Bahamian girl by accusing her of being "the culprit who had written the dirty word on the blackboard about Miss Sweeney: *lesbian*.") Black is black; no obvious deviation from racist stereotypes can suffice for the comfort or approval of whites like Susan Cole. ("I was here first, and I work here, and no goddam immigrant or cleaning woman or black son-of-a-bitch, nobody's gonna make me feel threatened and live like a victim in my own fucking country, province . . . in my city.")

We are given just a few lines that take us into the mind of the black man in a suit and tie, and nothing about his observation of her. He is, as far as we know, preoccupied with the fact that he's late for his interview. But in the short time they are together two crucial scraps of information about the woman are recorded: on the ring she wears "was the crest of Bishop Strachan," and "Danger came into her stomach, like the first signs of diarrhea." And that's it – hallelujah! From these two signals, the author-in-thin-disguise has constructed the story in our hands, about a graduate of a posh Toronto girls' school whose co-workers find her highfalutin and who hates an immigrant cleaning woman she suspects of being a lesbian; a story that begins with this woman he's called Susan Cole perched on a toilet she has been visiting all day because she has diarrhea; a story that centres on another elevator ride with a different black man – this one wearing a colourful windbreaker ("she has already painted a picture of his attire, and could pick him out of any police line-up with her eyes closed") and listening on his Walkman, she mistakenly assumes, to what else but "Rap!"; a story that ends with this polite college boy holding the door open for Susan Cole and then disappearing down the street like "a basketball star or a ballet dancer" or an object of impossible desire.

In "Beggars," we meet again our author-in-thin-disguise. He's in a crowded subway train, pressed up against a woman, and she is holding onto him for balance:

> "Sorry," she says.
> "Sorry," I say.
> But I am not sorry. She squeezes her eyes shut. Opens them, in an expression of friendship and forgiveness.... She closes her eyes again.... And I try to put her back, a half hour, or an hour-and-a-half, back into her house....

So this time it is clear. What we have is a man creating a character, imagining a story. It begins with close-up, in-her-skin physical detail – how as she wakes her cotton nightgown "is riding up along one leg, above her thigh," as anyone who has watched closely will know that nightgowns are inclined to do – and moves to what is on her mind and her early morning routine. It's an episode featuring her financial worries and her shower and the careful application of make-up and her unemployed husband who requires sex before she leaves for work. ("I have put her at forty years of age. Perhaps, thirty-nine. She is tall. About five feet, seven. And well-built.") At one point before he wakes up, "she looks down with distaste at her husband, so close to death, if she has a mind for it; and she wonders now, suffering her own suffocation, why she never gave her children a dolphin made of plastic. Or a whale. Or a fish." Why only "plastic ducks and plastic bears" for the children's bath? The killing of her husband is an idle fantasy, gone before the sentence is out.

Soon "the train jerks, coming to a stop. It is the first stop since I have made this woman's acquaintance." They are still pressed up against each other. Her eyes open and close once more:

> And then, like a woman in sleep that is not deep, she starts, tosses long strands of reddish brown hair out of her eyes, as she would coming out of the sea, and is immediately, immaculately, a different woman.... She is taken back, back for half an hour, or an hour-and-a-half, in her own mind....

This time she wakes to the necessity of killing a small cockroach that is crawling away from her face on a double mattress that lies on the hardwood floor. Again, "her nightgown was gathered at her waist." The new story about the woman's husband stretches out, intensified. The cockroaches multiply. She has left the bastard, four nights ago, following one of many vicious beatings, in which first he slaps her around. "She stood there, feeling the pain and humiliation deep down," but he was not "satisfied." Her reaction is not sufficient to appease him:

So, he began to beat her with his fists. He was in the ring again, fighting his first amateur bout.... He struck her with a right cross...and the man in front of him was dancing around, making him look clumsy and foolish before the screaming crowd. "Ya bum! Ya bum!" He could hear the boos now, five years later. And he hit her with a left hook.

It is an old story, this one. The husband's mix of desire and out-raged pride, his wife's passivity, his feeling that "the foe in front of him was absorbing all his toughness and meanness, all his power," leads finally to "delight" in a newly conceived form of violence. But she sees his smile, sees her own death coming:

And miraculously, the ring stopped its constricting, and began to expand back outwards. It became the room in which he was strangling her. It became as large as the house itself; larger, larger, until the entire neighbourhood was encompassed. And she could see life outside this arena of blows and insult and degra-dation.

She gets him in the testicles, breaking free at last. And all this is what she is thinking about as she kills the cockroaches in her apartment, "and this is what went through her mind as she stood in the crowded subway car, pressed by the man who was trying to read her thoughts . . . ."

The train stops, and our author-figure watches as she "comes alive from the corridors of her past she had been walking during its ride." She gets off: "And with her leaves a part of myself, for I had fashioned and created her in the image and lust of my desire this morning when there was nothing else on my mind." The story closes with his thinking of this woman as his "darling" and of "the fear that resides on women's faces," a theme he has returned to in a story that should answer for once and all the question that is always posed to writers: where do your stories come from anyway, where do you get your ideas?

In "Not So Old, But Oh So Professional," the author-figure is outed again in a Cabbagetown restaurant that he visits regularly to observe the prostitutes. A pimp passes by his table, asking to his astonishment, "'How's the writing racket?'" Our man takes one of the young prostitutes home with him, and they drink and they talk until morning. Desire is one thing, an admitted truth; but a writer's material and his human heart is another and more central to this story.

In "Just a Little Problem," the man's mother (she who because of her love must be obeyed) informs him by telephone that his much younger brother is coming to Toronto and that he is not to allow him to drink. This brother has been slowly killing himself with drugs and alcohol. The prohibition poses a serious problem, as the author-figure is himself something of a devoted booze-hound, as the reader will have easily detected by now; and his house is replete with good bottles that get emptied wherever he hides them. Besides, "in our way of doing things, to be able to drink is the sign of manhood. A man who can't hold his liquors is like a dog. Women despise him. Men call him a boy. And children pelt him with stones." This is a lovely, tender story. Like the next, penultimate story, "They're Not Coming Back," it takes us close to the question of death that hovers over the final story about the two old black men in cashmere coats, "The Cradle Will Fall."

With "They're Not Coming Back" we are again in the world of mothers. Claudette, the central character, has had a bad marriage and has lost her children. The pain of that loss is overwhelming. Her house is full of little notes left by a daughter, messages that speak cryptically to the pain and the bond that remain and that will haunt that daughter when her mother too is lost. Again, there is drink: Claudette "loved martinis and drank them in generous quantities. They were part of her sophistication." But now the drink and the pills are about her sorrow. And into this comes Claudette's own mother, gentle and protective and grieving over how Claudette has thrown her life away on a worthless man. "'Sleep. Sleep, my darling'" – it is all that is left to say.

Despite all of the pain and sexual violence and racism and recklessness that inhabit Austin Clarke's *There Are No Elders*, this is in many ways a joyful (and very funny) book. It is full of the zest of living and of writing well, of truly *seeing* both the self and others in the time we have:

> "Nevermindthat!"
> "Why never mind that?"
> "Nevermindthat!"

The bad is out there, in here. But there is also, abundantly, everything else. We need sometimes to "nevermind" the one in order to attend properly to the other, however mixed up they necessarily also are. Loving and hating, growing in wisdom and throwing it all away in the stupidity of our lives, are one story and also two – as the comic and the tragic, or Canada and the West Indies, or men and women, or childhood and old age, are one story and also two. *There Are No Elders*, as a claim, is debatable. "Is only old people," says Derek Walcott in the poem from which Austin Clarke extracts his title. Well, maybe so, and maybe not. Walcott again: "I am best suited to stalk like a white cattle bird/ on legs of sticks, with sticking to the Path/ between the canes on a district road at dusk." Throughout this fine book, the seasoned writer stalks, sticking to the Path that is also "between" paths, moving at full power between one consciousness or perspective and another, sticking and switching, hauling in his green crop. Bravo, Austin Clarke. The man has gotten through all the ice and snow and the shifting sand on legs that will last.

Leon Rooke
April 2007

Leon Rooke is the author of, among other books, *Oh!, Who Goes There, Fat Woman, Shakespeare's Dog, The Face of Gravity, A Good Baby, The Magician of Love, The Beautiful Wife,* and most recently a book of poems, *Hot Poppies.*

IF THE BOUGH BREAKS

Where they were, on the second floor of a building that squatted at the corner of Bay and Davenport, whose ground floor was taken up by a store that sold milk for five cents more than you could buy it in any supermarket, and beside which was a store that sold everything, these five women were chatting while two others sat in the hairdresser's chair. The hairdresser was a man. Christophe. A big, strong man with a black complexion, from Barbados. He had never learned French at school; had never visited the islands in the West Indies where French is spoken; but he understood what French meant in his business in this city, so he changed his name from Granville Da Costa the moment he graduated near the bottom of the class from the Marvel School of Hairdressing; went by bus to Montreal and stayed there for a long weekend, Labour Day weekend; and when he returned, by train, he had the name Christophe and a new accent. He called every customer, chérie, which came out as "cherry." He had two women working for him. They themselves had graduated from the Marvel School of Hairdressing, three months ago, near the top of their class.

On the front of the building, on the second floor where these five women were now sitting, emblazoned in lights, was CRISTOPHE'S SALO. The lights that formed the letter N, in "salon" never worked. But Christophe was known throughout the city as the best hairdresser, the only man, or woman, who knew how to "fix" black women's hair.

One woman had curlers and grease in her hair; another woman's hair was lathered in shampoo, so thick and rich, you could not tell her age, although she was the youngest in the salon. And the five waiting together were all over forty and well-dressed; and two of them had foreign cars parked below; after one hour, they had given up running down the stairs to put loonies into the meters.

The girl in the chair cried out, as the shampoo ran into her eyes, stinging her, "Are you trying to blind me Christophe? I'm too old to learn Braille, hear." She was a fourth-year student at the University. She was studying psychology. She was very good-looking. She came from a rich Barbadian family who owned a very small sugar cane plantation that grew sugar cane no longer. "I have theories to read."

"Cuddear, cherry!"

It was three o'clock, Thursday afternoon. They could hear the traffic below and the voices of people passing, for the windows facing the street were open for the breeze.

Christophe had forgotten to call the repairman to come and fix the two noisy air-conditioners, taped round their perimeter with electrical tape which his friend Cox, a plumber had left. So, the room was warm. And the five ladies were using the boxes of Kleenex, passing them from hand to hand, mopping their brows, their embroidered hankies already saturated. And the prospect of the ironing comb, not really a comb made of iron by a blacksmith as many used back in the West Indies, but its modern version, which performed the same function, making their hair "white," making their temples hot, threatening burns on their scalps, certainly singeing hair in the wrong places, all this made their waiting more uncomfortable than the patience they knew they must have each time they visited this salon, always too crowded, too slow, and too under-staffed. They had been Christophe's customers for years.

In with a whiff of wind which cooled the salon came voices of a quarrel below on the street. The room was quiet for a moment. Then, a siren screamed through the buzz of voices, and the humidity seemed to clutch the women's bodies, and cause them to breathe more heavily. The noise increased and it seemed as if the ambulance or the police cruiser was going to climb right up the flight of stairs and join them. And in fact, it did stop in front of the entrance. The five women ran to the windows.

There was a hiss. The sirens stopped. And the hissing sound lasted a few more moments. The two assistants dropped their instruments into some kind of liquid. They joined the others at the windows. Christophe continued fixing the young woman's hair.

There were three large windows. The lower half of each was pulled up. So the women could lean their bodies out, and see. And they could look at one another leaning out the three windows. It was not an ambulance. There were three police cars. Stopped in the middle of the road, blocking all traffic. The owner of the store who sold high-priced milk came out to meet the policemen. They had left their car doors open. The women could hear the three radios crackling. The six policemen had their guns drawn. In the distance, coming towards them, was another cruiser, flashing in red speed and urgency.

"I bet you," one woman said, "it's some black man in there."

"And not eighteen yet," another said.

The policemen and the store owner were now inside the store.

"These people!" one of the assistants said. "I was walking through the Eaton Centre one night, and just as I take up my parcel with the things I bought in it, and paid for, all of a sudden I feel this hand on my shoulder, and when I turn round...."

"Blasted people, eh?"

Two of the policemen came back out. Between them was a young white girl. No more than sixteen. They took her to a car, and put her to sit in the back seat, while the other four officers exchanged words which the women could not hear; and then they too got into their cruisers, and drove off. The few men and women who had stopped to look, walked on. One man took a red box from his pocket, extracted a cigarette and lit it. He walked at a faster pace. A bus was coming. The wind was blowing again. The store owner came back outside with a broom, sweeping the sidewalk; and they could see because of the stains from chopping meat and pork and roasts on his white apron that covered his body from his neck to his thighs, that he sold other things than milk.

"What do you think they got her for?"

"Shoplifting."

"They begin young."

"Well, it was a good thing," the assistant continued, "that I had kept my receipt that Friday night. It was the Friday before the Caribana parade, and I was thinking of stopping at the kiosk-thing to buy a Lotto, 'cause I had had a dream the night before. But before I could walk more than two feet from the counter where I had bought the pantihose, this blasted man's hand on my shoulder. I look round. And staring me in my face is this blasted man. Security guard. Accusing me. Of something. Say I shoplifting. Well, I not ashamed to tell you, I let-go some bad words in his arse, that caused all the people in the Eaton Centre to stare at me. These blasted people, eh?"

"How old you think that girl is?"

"I could only see her head."

"I wonder if she have a mother?"

"From the back, which is all I could see, I would put her at sixteen."

"So young? And to have a record?"

"She's sixteen, as you say. She can breed."

4

"Christ, waiting here on Chris, my mind all the way up in Pickering, wondering if *my* child went home straight from school. We moved up in Pickering to get away from crime and violence down here, but child, I tell you, up there isn't any better than down in Jane-Finch corridor, if you ask me."

"In the weekend *Star*, did you read the thing about teenage pregnancies?"

"Wonder what time Chris intends to get to my hair? Four o'clock, and school must be out a long time."

"What happened?"

"You mean the article?"

"No. The security guard and the pantihose."

"I looked him straight in his face. The whole store watching me now. I faced him and I said, in my best manner, 'Let me tell you something nigger-man.'"

"You called him that?"

"Was he black?"

"What was his complexion?"

"If you want to," I tell him, "you could put your hand in my bag. But let me tell you something. When you put your hand in my bag, I am going to take off my shoe, and *drive* it right into your two blasted testicles."

"No!"

"His complexion was what?"

"Not black."

"And you called him a nigger-man?"

"He was a white man."

"No!"

"And what happened?"

"He didn't say another word to me."

"*No!* But the teenaged pregnancies is what I want to know about."

"I didn't read the newspapers that weekend."

"Anybody have that article? Joyce, you think you still have it? You clips things from the *Star*."

"Was in the *Globe*."

"I don't take the *Globe*. The *Star* is my speed."

"Mr. Chris, how much longer before you getting-round to fixing my hair? I have a child at home waiting on me."

"And a husband."

"Had!"

"You divorced, cherry? I didn't know you and the old-man had break-up, cherry?"

"In name only, Mr. Chris, a husband in name only."

"That girl, that we just see being arrested by the police, I am sure that they're going to take her down in that station and make that girl's life miserable, and they may even do...."

"Do what to her? Do what to her? What you mean by miserable?"

"Child, every other day in the newspapers there's stories about the police and women they have in their cruisers."

"But that child, though."

"She's sixteen. She can breed."

"You mean rape."

"Who said anything about rape?"

"Sexual assault. Sexual assault is the name for it nowadays. Everything nowadays is sexual assault."

"Growing up in the West Indies...."

"You're a damn liar!"

"How can you accuse me before you hear what...?"

"What you're about to say? I already know it, before you even say it. You were about to say that growing up in the West Indies, we didn't have anything such as what we witnessing nowadays in this place."

"Well, how the hell could you know what I...?"

"Because I know you. And I know the West Indies. And I...."

"You know too blasted much. You must be working *obeah*, that you can read my mind."

The five women were sitting again. The wind came through the windows in a slight gust, and for a moment, it was as if Christophe had fixed the air-conditioners.

"Every year. Child, when you see Christmas come and the 28th is here, I longing for home. But I won't go home *before* Christmas. Christmas isn't Christmas unless you have a tree and snow."

"Child, all over the West Indies nowadays, is trees, and *real* Christmas trees too! Not the artificial ones we had in our days!"

"Snow, too!"

"Snow, too? What the hell I hearing?"

"You didn't know? Didn't hear? For *years* now, the tourist board people in Barbados been importing snow from Canada. For years now."

"You don't mean the Tourisses from Canada? You not referring to white people?"

"I am no prejudice. I talking about the snow. I understand it comes from Toronto, whiching...."

"*And* Montreal!"

"Whiching is the best snow in North America."

"Who's next, my cherries?"

Christophe removed the plastic bib from the neck of the woman who was now almost two hours in his chair. The smoke from his cigarette rose gently. He put the cigarette to his lips; pursed his lips as if he was about to kiss the woman dismounting clumsily from the high chair; put the cigarette in the glass ashtray, and said, "Who's next, my cherries?"

The five women looked at one another. They had had lunch together at the Four Seasons Hotel nearby. They had had two

7

martinis each. And when they arrived, giggling, after discussing their children and their families and their husbands, as they did each time they had lunch, once in two weeks, they were fortified through food and drink, to wait the long wait in the old hard plastic-bottomed chairs. The plastic made their dresses stick to their bottoms and they could feel the lumps where the upholstery had collapsed against their soft well-cared-for skin.

"You have a child coming from school soon. You go."

"Charmaine can look after herself, man."

"You're not concern about that little girl walking the street and going home to an empty house with all this *worthlessness* you read about in Toronto?"

"Well, child, I would never allow my Suzianne to enter an empty house. Nor go to the mall with her friends. Some o' these friends, I tell you."

"Charmaine's the same age as that child the police had downstairs a few minutes ago."

"Talking about bringing up children. Do you believe we bring up our children better than *them?*"

"Well, you getting me mad as hell now! The evidence speaks for itself." One amongst them, who had been quiet, now spoke up. "How you could compare *them* with we, with us? The facts speak for themselves! If it is only once, in my twenty-something years living in Toronto, I have lived to see the day when a police go in a store and don't bring out a black boy or a black girl, but a damn white girl. And all o' you spending your time taking up for that girl? I haven't heard nobody amongst you, in the two or three hours we been sitting down waiting for Mr. Chris to fix our hair, nobody, not *one* of you haven't uttered a word in support of the police! Not one of you!"

"Wait! She fooping a police?"

"She's a married woman, child."

"Her husband would break her arse if he *only* heard!"

"Are you sleeping with one o' Metro's finest, on the sly, girl?"

"The girl is a little whore!"

"She was unfaired by the police."

"Not the police. The man who own the store is who called the police. Blame *him*. He could be the son-of-a-bitch."

"Who's next? Cherries? Who's next?"

"We're talking business, man."

"Just a minute, Chris, man."

"The fact that it was a white girl and not one of ours, well, that answers the question. We raise ours better than *them*."

"We had just moved to Pickering, in the house we're living in now, and it was a day like this, in late July; no, it must have been in August, 'cause we had just come back from watching the Caribana parade on University Avenue, and...."

"You see? You see? Christ, they couldn't let us parade on University, 'cause University Avenue is too good for black people, so they moved us down beside the Lake, where nobody can't see us, whilst they leave right-wingers like the Shriners to walk all over this city on tricycles as if they are blasted kids! You see? You see?"

"Nevermindthat!"

"Why never mind that?"

"Nevermindthat! We had just moved into Pickering and my daughter was nine, my son was six and my other daughter was eight, and we had just got home from sweating-up ourselves in the Caribana parade, and it was so hot and we had nothing cool in the house to drink, so me and my husband...."

"The cop you was seeing on the sly?"

"And fooping with? I did-hear that."

"Fuck you."

"Me, child? I can't do it by myself!"

"Was nothing in the house cool to drink, as I was saying, so we send the eight-year-old to the convenience store, just across the street, in the mall to buy a large bottle o' pop, 'cause we had just got a bottle o' Mount Gay from a girl friend who had gone home on holiday and me and Percy opening this forty-ounce and waiting for the child to come back from the plaza, and when we hear the shout, these blasted sirens going like hell in front our house, and four police in three cars jump out and my child in the back seat of one o' them police cars, *handcuff.* Well, Bejesus Christ, you shouldda seen how my husband *react*!"

"No!"

"Good dear!"

"Oh, God! This happened to you?"

"And you never mentioned a word of this before?"

"Some of the things you have to keep to yourself, eh?"

"No. Not a' eight-year-old child, handcuff, in the back of a police cruiser! *No!*"

Christophe struck three matches before he could light his mentholated cigarette. The smoke shot through his nostrils without sound, in two long piercing white streams. The cars outside the windows were moving fast. Horns were blown in exasperation. And the women could hear a few complaining voices. When the cars passed they could hear the footsteps of people on the street, and the scratching of the broom as the store owner swept the sidewalk; and then they heard the scratching of a match on a box, and the inhaling of the first lung-full of cigarette. It was one of the two assistant women hairdressers, smoking a Salem.

"Go on. Pass her a fresh Kleenex to dry her eyes."

"*My* eight-year-old. We send her to Sunday school every Sunday. From the time she was two, every Sunday as the Lord said, she was in that Sunday school class. We send her to piano lessons from the time she was five and last year, taking the advice of a friend of ours, she's been taking ballet lessons, and...."

"*That's* the way we bring up our children!"

"And her ballet teachers at the Ballet School just down there on a side-street near Church, her ballet teachers tell us that the child have a future in pirouettes. And, don't laugh, that August afternoon at five, four police have *my* child handcuff, in the back of a police cruiser and all the neighbours looking out and pointing. When we moved up there, four months pass before the one on our left said a word in regards to good morning or good evening; and the afternoon my husband brought home the new car, you should have seen them staring from behind their curtains. We shouldn't have those things. We shouldn't live the way *they* live. We shouldn't."

"What your husband did?"

"Pass her another Kleenex."

"It's too sad. It was too sad that August afternoon. It was too sad. And too shameful. I can't talk about it, no more."

"Don't then. We know everything you were going to say. It happens to all of us. We know. You don't have to say any more, 'cause it is the history and the experience of each and every one of us in this room."

"Well, who's next?"

"My mind is still on that white girl."

"Are you her god-mother?"

"She's a child."

"A child? She's a white girl. And she is the daughter of the four police in those three cruisers who molested this woman's eight-year-old daughter and handcuff her. She is the daughter of that landlord who didn't rent me that musty, stinking basement apartment years ago, in 1961 on Walmer Road. She is the daughter of the woman at the Eaton Centre who had the security guard come up in my face accusing me of shoplifting, a decent person like me.

She is the future mother of all the racists we come across in this city. She is just herself."

"Is a hard sentence, though."

"At least, she's a thief."

"I won't put that judgement on her, though, 'cause as I said, when my husband saw those four police having my daughter in the back of that cruiser, handcuff, well...."

"Sins of the fathers, my dear. Sins of the fathers. I didn't say it, and like bloody hell, I didn't cause it! You can find it in your Bible, if you ever read the Bible."

"And what sins have we committed in this place, since all of us were living here, coming from various parts of the West Indies? Name me one. Go right ahead and name me *one*. Name me one. The only sins we committed in this place, is obeying the blasted law. And from what I see, there is one law for us, and one for *them*."

"We raise our kids better than them."

"There isn't no argument 'gainst that, as far's I concerned."

"We're sitting down here in this hair-dressing place, in at Christophe, five middle-class bitches with not one worry in the world, except if our husbands going-crawl home before three in the morning, cattawouling."

"And with some o' these same white bitches!"

"Look at the five of us! I dress well. She dresses well. You dress well. Look at the dress that one is wearing. Five well-off bitches like us, with two-car garage, educated, decent and have more education that most women, than the average Canadian white woman. And with *all* this, we have to walk-'bout Toronto with our head down, and...."

"Shit! Not *my* head!"

"Christ, I looks them right in their blasted eye!"

"I know, I know. Individually. But I'm speaking as a rule, as a general rule. You know what I mean. Back home, we'd be ruling the roost. We'd be women with men and husbands that make decisions and run things. But here, if it isn't some bloody parking-lot attendant who hasn't been here for six months, and can't even talk English, if it not some woman at the Eaton Centre, and don't mention Holt Renfrew or some o' them places in Yorkville Village, if it is not some damn racist cop, if it isn't some woman in a beat up Toyota, while you or she are driving a BMW, or I behind the wheel of my husband's Benz, *anything*, any-blasted-body, we always have to explain *some* thing to them. Explain ourselves. Explain."

"My husband been driving a 68 Chev for ten years and would come home and curse *me*, and say how the cops in Toronto are the best. Last year, the son-of-a-bitch got his hand on some insurance money from a policy we had take out fifteen years ago, and he bought this second-hand Mercedes Benz I just referred to. It spends more time in the garage round the corner than parked in front of our house. He bought a note book from Grand & Toy. A black little note book. Guess what he puts down in that little black book?"

"'Course, he puts down the mileage!"

"Or the miles!"

"What's the difference? Miles is mileage!"

"Not in my book, cherry," Christophe said.

"Every week. After ten o'clock. When he gets off the Don Valley Parkway. A cop. A copy in his arse! Three times a week, a cop pulls him over. As an average."

"They want him."

"Sending him a message."

"To go back to the 68 Chev."

"And here we are worrying about a little white girl that got picked up for shoplifting from a Mac's Milk. Ain't that something? We five black bitches, in a black hairdressing place, sitting down this lovely summer afternoon, worrying over a little white thief!"

"Harsh, though! Too harsh, cherry," Christophe said.

"How would *you* know? You ever given birth?"

"You don't have to be a woman to know that."

"A woman is a woman."

"I suppose you gonna say next that we have the same *thing* between our legs!"

"I wasn't getting personal, I was barely stating that a woman is a woman, and a mother is a mother, and...."

"A child is a child. Is that what you saying? That the one out there a few hours ago, arrested by the police, is the *same* as my eight-year-old? I bet you. I bet you *anything* that they took her a little way down the street from Mac's Milk, and let her go, and that poor man who owns the store will never get satisfaction for whatever it is she took."

"What she took?"

"What she could've taken to justify the way the police came, with sirens blaring?"

"That's a strange comment coming from a black woman like you! With your eight-year-old?"

"What was her crime? We sitting down here all this time, and nobody knows what is her crime?"

"*Stealing!*"

"Who's next? This is my last time, cherries!"

"And being white."

"Suppose, just suppose, they took her away for her own good. Suppose it's the owner of the store down those stairs who did that to her?"

They could hear the footsteps coming up the stairs. Another customer, probably. The breeze was cooler now. No one snatched a white tissue from the jumbo-sized Kleenex box. The thin smoke from Christophe's cigarette moved in their faces. One woman sneezed.

"Bless you!"

"Sinus?"

"Allergies."

"Is these blasted cigarettes Christophe smoking!"

The footsteps stopped. All of them turned to look. It was a young white girl. No more than sixteen. They continued looking, not speaking, not believing their eyes. In the short silence that was heavy as the earlier humidity in the room, they went back over the scene down below on the street, the police cruisers and the policemen with their hands on their guns, and the short store owner in his stained white apron sweeping the dust from the entrance of his store. And when they saw her, a gasp came from their mouths, and they were paralyzed for a moment. And then they all rushed to the little child. A newspaper was in her hand. She was sixteen perhaps, as in their recollection; but her appearance rendered her helpless, unprotected and much smaller, a child in their eyes; and she seemed unable to move another step up the stairs. She had stopped at the round, hand-polished newel ball at the head of the banister. Christophe had tied a red ribbon round the newel last Christmas Eve, as decoration, and it had remained there ever since.

Her face was red. Red from the colour of the blows that had struck her face. Her lips were thicker than the lips of any of the five women. Her face had no expression. At first, the women could not tell whether it was fright or shame.

They were sure that what they would hear from her mouth would be tales of pain, of assault. The thought went through each of their minds at the same piercing moment and, with five slight variations, their minds sped to their homes where they could see their own children. She looked as if she could be drugged. As if someone had given her something to drink that contained a drug. They did not believe she had taken it herself, by herself. They believed she was too innocent, too nice a little girl. She was a child. A newspaper was in her hand.

"Lisa!"

She held the afternoon *Star*.

Christophe said the name; and said it two more times. The third time he called her name, it was astonishment turning to unbelief. "*Lisa?*"

"You know this girl?"

"She's his niece. She delivers my paper."

"The corner store man?"

"Mr. Macdonald's niece, Lisa. She lives with him."

"This girl's in trouble, Chris, you can't see that? We have to do something for this poor child, man."

"Come, come," one of the women said. "Come."

"Ask her what happened?"

"Not now, man, not now. This is an emergency."

They half-carried her, surprised at her solid weight, to the chair where the last customer had sat; and they turned the tray with the shampoos and the pins and the curlers and the straightening agents aside, and they placed two soft cushions on the black leatherette bottom, to give growth and height to her body; and someone in the meantime was filling a sink with hot water; and the steam was rising higher than Christophe's cigarette smoke; he was holding a cigarette at the corner of his mouth, with one eye closed against the sting of the mentholated smoke; and one woman stood behind Lisa and held her gently against the hard black leatherette back of the chair; and one woman stood on each side, rubbing a hand over Lisa's chest which was rising and falling as if she were running from something, while the remaining two women took turns testing the heat of the water pouring out of the hot water tap, soaking white towels and testing the heat against their faces and gauging Lisa's ability to withstand the steam.

The hot towel made her start. And close her eyes. And it was then that they saw the tears on her beautiful skin. The towel moved over her cheeks, and she winced. She closed her eyes each time the towel touched her, but they could see the blueness of her ears. They could see the holes pierced in her ears, for earrings. They could see her teeth, pink against the strong fluorescent light pouring down from above; and when they shifted their position, running the warm towel round her neck, her teeth became sparkling white. They could see a scratch at the bottom of her neck. "Take off her dress." She still had the newspaper in her left hand.

"Not the whole dress, she's a child, after all. Just lower the blouse.

But someone raised the hem of her dress, and they saw it. For a moment, they stopped passing the lukewarm towel round her neck. They took the newspaper out of her hand, and handed it to Christophe, and he dropped it on the floor. And the women who stood at the back of the tall leatherette chair, kept their hands on her wrists and on her left shoulder. Christophe stubbed his cigarette into a jar of hair pomade. The grease embedded the cigarette into itself. It was blood on her leg. On one leg.

"*Blood?*"

"Jesus Christ!"

"It's blood, all right."

The five women thought of their children, daughters and sons. The five women thought of their husbands. And one by one, but together in their fear and in their horror at the spectacle and what they knew the spectacle could mean, they went back over all those times, when their own children had been left with uncles and brothers-in-law, with close friends of their families, with their own husbands, fathers of their children, and they dared not travel back with too much memory and clarity and honesty. It was blood on her leg.

No one wanted to ask the question.

They knew the answer without having to pose it, even to themselves. They knew it could be one thing only. One cause. One kind of violence. It was the violence they knew. That they had lived with from birth. Pain and blood. Blood and pain, in a combination of joy, of sorrow, of natural function, and for those blessed with fertility, the pain and blood of giving birth.

"Why does it always have to be so?" said the woman whose daughter had been handcuffed. "Why does it have to be so, all the time?"

Her eyes were filled with tears. And she made no effort to hide her disconsolation. She was now holding the child's body, in her arms, and was rocking back and forth, her tears falling into the blonde hair of the child, who was now sobbing, and who had in all this time, not spoken a word. "Why is it always this way with women? And for women?"

"Call the police."

"Who have the number for the police? I never had to call the police before."

"Call any number. Call *all* the numbers. One must be the police. Call 7-6-7!"

"That is S-O-S on the telephone dial."

"So call the police."

SHIP, SAIL! SAIL FAST!

She did not take the taxi through the unknown streets to see him off. It had been his first visit to the small town, where she lived in a place popular among students with a dog which she'd found and kissed and slept in bed with; and before he had finished dinner, she removed her plate with half the food eaten, and placed it on the floor for the dog to lap up, and relish. He had stopped eating after that. He had not spoken another word. Now, he had fifteen minutes, through this meandering slow town, in the taxi driven by a man who did not seem to know the town, to catch the train. It was not the last train, but his anger made it seem like that, and helped to justify his fury and his nervousness, and his dislike bordering on hatred for the innocent, slow taxi driver. They passed through the streets he had walked two days ago, hand in hand with her, comfortable in his new love, anxious for the bed that would follow the cool, long uninteresting stroll beside the river, along desolate streets with solid buildings on them where men and women who looked like students moved just as slowly as this taxi; he refused to be impressed by the beauty which people say you can find in small towns. He did not like small towns.

He felt like a man escaping custody. But during his incarceration in the small, dog infested room, he had grown accustomed to the plastic cover on the toilet bowl which he had to sit sideways on; to the shower which beat against the sides of its tin enclosure; to the dining table which his knees knocked against, causing the legs to buckle and almost fold and toss the food untouched to the dog, as it was a folding table made for playing cards; and the bed made of three found mattresses of three difference sizes, which slid each time he mounted them, and her. He had got accustomed, like a man who has acknowledged that he has to spend time against his wishes, in a confined space, getting to know the restriction and abiding with it, because there is no other way.

"How much farther?"

"We'll be there soon."

He looked at the cluttered dashboard that had more instruments on it than he had ever seen in a taxi in the city; and was searching for the one that told the time and speed.

"Why are you doing twenty-five?"

"In this town, the limit is thirty, sir."

"So, why are you...?"

"Can't go faster, in this town."

They were on a street where the buildings were large and empty, and he thought of olden times when sugar or flour or saw-dust must have been made in that building, and the streets were crowded and the traffic moved like this creeping taxi, as the townsfolk traveled in polished, scrubbed carriages, with rubbed-down horses.

On his left was the vast body of water the colour of lead; they called it The Lake, but he had never seen a lake this size; and close by, to the side of the street, was a ship that stretched for two blocks, looming, and he thought of disaster. What was she doing now, left alone in the angry farewell of silent words? Was she kissing the dog to make up for his anger? Or kicking the dog to transfer her disappointment with the man who had entered her life just as two ships pass each other in fog or falling snow? He thought of the ship which was large enough to enter oceans, faltering in its arrival at this port, and hitting a large rock, with its invisible dimensions below the surface, and crumpling; and voices raised in terror and frustration.

When he had seen her body, and the softness of her limbs, her breasts which his anxious hands covered; and he felt her body shudder and then collapse, as his touch became lighter, moving over her not quite brown, not quite white, cool skin, she had held her eyes closed against his passion; but her body kept shaking. In her eyes was something like terror, something that said she was fearful of the ecstasy she had started to enjoy.

And he'd told himself then, that he knew.

A horn sounded. He did not know about trains. It could be the train signal getting ready to leave. He could not see any building which looked like a train station. But in these small towns, the station could be a shed. Buried behind the two-storied brown-painted buildings which flanked the street. The street was quite crowded. And the slow-moving cars reminded him that it was Sunday; and he guessed that no one here took a train on a summer afternoon on a Sunday, preferring to be in Sunday school, or walking beside the unmoving Lake with dog and kid and girlfriend and lover, watching the ship that has not moved in years.

"Here we are!"

And the ride he was taking with his eyes and imagination has come to this sparse end, with men and women loitering outside the station, and the train huffing and chugging. The ticket seller pauses to ask a woman how was her trip to the big city, and whether her son is still in the hospital, when the horn goes again and he wants to pull the ticket seller from behind her cage and spread her on the floor.

"Have a nice trip sir, there is no hurry as the train ain' going nowhere, it just got in and I'll tell you when you are to board, if you want a coffee just around the corner or potato chips or a pop you can sit here then, and I'll see you and tell you."

She is lying on the three-tiered bed and her eyes are soaked in water and they seem like soft slits of passion and they are looking into the eyes of the white-haired dog who looks like an African albino through a meeting of two bloods, and she asks the dog why her man does not like him, that he is only a dog.

He sits by a window. The train cuts through a village on the outskirts of the town. And he can see the barbecues belching smoke; and a man with thick pieces of dead animal in his hand in a bowl with forceps. The train is going through the backyard of village after village. The roses are still red. The green is the grass on which the children fooled the rules of football, touching the football and touching the grass. And then there is only corn. In the city the corn is already dead. But in this rumbling, inhospitable cutting through the privies of these homes, the corn raises its head and can reach a tall man to his shoulder, hiding secret and compelling crimes, unseen by the eyes of the woman, old as an aunt, who sits on a collapsible chair and breathed in the perfume of the red dead animal. Beef.

Years ago, he would walk through the ears of corn, and rip the blond hair from the stalk when no one was looking and turn himself into a European with a silk moustache. Or if he was reading a book about buccaneers, make a beard like Sinbad the Sailor, and mow through the waves of the green and the corn and come out at the end, miscalculated like a pilot who had not learned his lessons, on the compass. A wrecked frigate.

"*Ship, sail.*"

"*Sail, fast.*"

"*Hommany men 'pon deck?*"

"*Twenty!*"

"*Give me twenty grains o' corn, you idiot! I only have three in my hand. How-haw-haw!*"

Five years after that evening when the sky was golden, as if there could be autumn in the island, and the sea, not a lake, was blue and white with the waves like the moustache of old Englishmen, she held his hand, and led him into the ocean of corn, where there was no current and no neighbours, where the trade winds could not reach, with the girl his only rudder, leading him into the valley of information and learning; and it must have been three minutes at the most, but three minutes filled with a lifetime of the mystery of this young girl's experience; his hand was trembling; and he thought she was taking him into this deepness to continue, she and he, the children's game. "Ship, sail! Sail fast!" It was he who had told her five nights before, when their school books had been put under the table for the weekend, "Twenty! Twenty men 'pon deck!"

"You little idiot!"

Now, the train has moved from the crowded yards with the small swimming pools, many of them raised above the lawns, with a ladder for a midget taking the shaking steps from the grass to the brink of disaster. It was the woman who had told him, just as he came out of the small shower walled-in by tin, where each drop sounded like a cataract, it was the woman who had told him, "Last summer, you know? Ten children drowned in swimming pools, the round ones, you know? This summer, and it's early in summer, August only, you know? Already thirteen fallen off step-ladders into the water, and drowned. The yards are larger. And the pools are dug into the green ground. It is very peaceful. It is Sunday afternoon, and no children are splashing in them. The corn comes right up to the kitchen garden bed in a corner of the paled backyard far from the pool, and he can see green tomatoes and some red, lettuce and other green things too far in the distance to name; he can see moustaches and beards on the corn. He wonders who were the first boys and girls, men and women, who ran through these green tunnels, hiding from danger; and who rode these green rails hiding from the inhabitants of the other country across the vast body of water? He had forgotten to ask the man the name of the lake. And in the book about the town, he had not reached that paragraph of its history.

The fields are running beside the train. They have the same speed. But he does not know the miles per hour. Two passenger cars and a truck come into his view on the right side, the farther side of the window. He pushes the shade up. They are beside him now, abreast, well within range. If he had a gun with power with a scope glass for accuracy, the cars and the truck would be brought into his sight, and *pow!*, with just one shot he could explode them. In his mind he aims, using the cigarette in his mouth as the rifle; but the smoke clouds his aim, so he exchanges this for the pencil he was using to write the entry under Sunday the 6th in his diary; and all of a sudden, the two cars and the truck are left behind in the rumbling of the train as it goes into a bend. The fields of corn are running beside this monster of iron.

And in them he sees the figure of a woman. Jane. He knows her name, because her name is the name of her plight. Her clothes were originally white, long and flowing over her legs which have caused so much pain and brutality and loving longing, and which have become the legs of any man assuming he was white. Jane is running beside the train. Her eyes are balls of horror, for in them he can see himself, without having seen her in that large yard on the other side of the body of water; can feel the cow-skin rip into her soft black back, the skin was no longer beautiful and black. A painting of barbed wire with thick powerful brush-strokes of red became her back. And she was the one who carried the largest bale of cotton, the largest collection of twigs, the largest of her seven children on her back. Her strong legs keep her abreast of the train, and her arms reach to the side of the train, where the short steps are, the same size as the step-ladder from which the thirteen children, not her children, not her cousins, fell into the raised, plastic swimming pools in the first short part of this summer. But with all her strength and desperation to jump on board, the train is still too fast for her agility.

Jane walked the hundred miles from the place across the water, without knowing how to swim, without knowing how to read the geography of the map, and all she knew was that the map had a meaning less intractable than geography and theodolites and compasses. The sun this Sunday afternoon is crisp and warm. Jane walked during the night, and slept like a big city bagwoman wherever her bodily strength exhausted her mind that held this promise of walking through the endless corn fields, beside the iron rails of this monster taking him away from the woman with the dog to the big city where no corn grows.

No cotton grows on the streets of the big city. Only a sign on a store on Yonge Street, and racks outside in the whirling wind, that say *Au Coton*. It is not the same cotton that Jane knew and lived through, and nearly died of. And just before Jane grows small and smaller in the disappointed distance, he sees the large black body of a man, naked down to his shorts, covered in perspiration. Jane's husband, Jim. And even though Jim cannot stand beside the road and raise his finger, and cajole the driver of a car to slow down and stop, he understands the protocol of catching rides. He sent Jane, a woman, to do his dirty finger-raising business. It was like that back in that yard in the other place across the body of water, when chickens and ducks, pigs and cows, and some snakes, roamed in a greater freedom of space than even he and Jane; and in that time, it was he who understood that a little mistake, a word said under the breath but loud enough for Mas'r to hear; the misappropriation of one of those freed hens in the yards; the miscalculation in the pouring of molasses for the horse and jackass, leaving too deep a bottom in the bottom of the pail; and his ignorance of mathematics and addition, but his proficiency with subtraction: twenty hams was put in the smoke-filled shed with the hickory leaves and the smoke broke out as if the whole goddamn place was on fire, Mas'r; and he said, under his breath, but too loud, Amma wish this goddamn place were going up in flame with these hams; but when he checked their smoking and their curing, one was gone. One gone! These two words became like a bell in the night, like a boot at the door, like a tap on the shoulder in a crowd, like the leather in the boot of the Gestapo, all over that land across the body of water. "One gone!" And dogs barked. Lights came on. Lanterns were carried. Dogs yelped, tasting the sweetness of blood. Whips were cracked for suppleness. And for length. And for deadliness. And men jumped on the backs of horses. Rifles and pistols were taken from their shelves, already oiled and ready for use. Bullets and shots were fired for practice in the air. And the small children, who knew those two words, laughed in their sleep, and wished, and wished. So that small miscalculation of arithmetic; and how was he to know, since no one had sat him down under the tree in the large yard, after his endless chores, to say, "One and one is two. Two and two is four. One from four is t'ree!" And for the love of his body; and for the love of his woman, and the love she bore him, he sent her forward, he pushed her forward, to take her rightful place of leadership, and she took and endured the sting of justice. It was a chastisement he could no longer bear. It was a punishment his black body held no unmarked area the size of a postage stamp to endure. That is why Jane came closer from the deep green patch of corn to hail the train.

He can see the man's disappointment. And the man's shame. For the man knew he was a man, even in the circumscribed circumstance of his life and of his woman's life. But he had no power to behave as a man. As the way he knew, if he were living in a different land, he was to behave. It was surprising that the man naked down to his shorts, torn and tattered from catching them against branches and barbed wire and the teeth of howling dogs, perhaps the almost deadly flight of a bullet; his clothes in the same condition as his woman's, it was surprising that he did not take his failure out on his woman and beat her in the full sight of the disappearing train.

"Never get tired of that scenery," the conductor said, punching a hole in the ticket. "Ya know. Years and years I been making this trip. In summer, winter, the fall and spring. And ya know. Always grabs my attention just to look out and see the things and the fields. Interesting, ain't it? He gives back the ticket, takes another from his pocket and places it above the seat. He does the same thing two seats beyond. Those two tickets are of a different colour. So, the colour must mean destination. Did Jane have a colour scheme for her hoped destination? Could Jim have told her what to choose? "Tell ya something," the conductor says, sitting in the opposite seat. "You seem to be a sensible gentleman, educated I would say. And I hope you take this the right way, but I would swear that in them fields o' corn, there's people living. I don't mean living as against dead, you understand. What I mean is this. There could be people in them fields carrying on a life like you and me. With differences of course. If you see what I mean! You ever seen it that way?"

"Could be."

They sit in silence, and the passing of time coincides with and runs beside the scenery they are watching.

"Well, have a good trip for the rest o' the way. Been good talking to ya."

He moves away, down the shaking corridor. The tune he is humming is barely recognizable, *Georgia on my mind....*

Why were there no mile posts beside railroad tracks so a man can tell how far he has traveled? Or how fast? It was so strange that you had to be in the carriage, the cage, the hub, or was it the *caboose*, to see where you were going. He is getting tired, and the monotony of the speed measured against the lasting green fields is beginning to dull his mind and his attention, just like the sensation in a plane, looking through the window shaped like a toilet seat, at clouds that bury the bulk of the plane and come harmless and dangerously close. He is not the kind of man who could slump into a seat, take out a paperback book and read, then fall asleep. Or talk to the stranger beside him. What would he say to this un-known man? Normally, he closes his eyes and pretends to be invisible. Or asleep. But during this trip, an escape from the woman who loved kissing the dog, and kissing him afterwards with the same lips, escaping from the dog as much as from the woman, he has pressed his head against the plate-glass window and the images of his conscience strike against the cool glass; and he sees the half-dressed Jane and her naked husband, Jim.

Now the train is beside water. And he thinks of that childhood, years ago in the sun, when there was only water at the end of his reaching eyes, wherever he looked. *Ship sail, sail fast!* There were ships, many ships; ships with sails bringing cod fish from Newfoundland; and the crows of the sea, those carrion-eating birds were numberless on the decks like albatrosses; and when the crows regain their dignity and sail away from the rotting, rotten fish, all that is left are the bodies of men and women. He cannot see the faces of these men. He cannot see the faces of these women. Only their skin and bones, no more covered with the salty delicious flesh of the cod fish but with its bones and white scabs and greyish skin, like the sin of age and disease and withering sickness. Every Saturday morning, his mother soaked a saucepan full of that cod from the Banks of Newfoundland, and after hours of softening the flesh, removed the bones, scrubbing away the white and the grey from the slab of cod no thicker than the cover of his green-backed exercise book, in which he wrote exercises in English composition: *The boy stood on the burning deck!*; and then the fresh small tomatoes grown in plots that were miniatures of the fields he passes on this train; and the lard oil, the sickened thin cod came alive in taste and deliciousness, as she poured it thick and richer after her operation, all over the thick, cloiding dish made from corn, dried and shelled and husked and ground by hand in Mr. Thorpe's Corn Grinding machine; and called it cou-cou. They told him when he left the island where this feast was manufactured, that cou-cou was from Africa; and now, in this body of water through which the train passes, over it, on a bridge, that past is bridged by the memory, and he can see those dying bodies left by the carrion-eating birds. Amongst them, there is no Jane. That was not a name she was christened with in Africa. There is no one called Jim. But he knows no African names. Once, in a fit of anger, he erased the name his mother told him he was given, while she stirred the okras into the slippery pot with the ground corn, and put in its place And large X. But X means nonentity. X means illiteracy. X marks the spot. Once, in the cod fish sauce thickened with tomatoes and fresh eschalots, he found a bone the shape of an X. It did not hide any mystery. So, he spent the afternoon, roaming through the village sucking it, as the boys played cricket; as the girls played rounders and as the men drank rum. His mother was at home reading *Revelations,* chapter 13. She loved *Revelations.* She loved Chapter 13. And she loved the first verse most of all. A crumbling, dried cross, or an X, depending upon his haste or impatience to read the verse five times each night, marked the spot. *And I stood upon the sand of the sea, and saw a beast rise up out of the sea, having seven heads and ten horns, and upon his horns ten crowns, and upon his heads the name of blasphemy.* They were surrounded by water, the Caribbean Sea or the Atlantic Ocean depending upon which hill he sat on and watched the sea. And later in the fading day, at dusk, the boys and the girls gathered in a circle, and played the game, *Ship, sail; sail fast!* Later still, the same night, the mothers and his mother sat in the backdoor looking out into the yard filled with sleeping chickens and ducks and centipedes, and his mother held them all in thrall, "Once upon a time, there was a horse that had seven heads, and ten foots, and my God, one dark night as I walking home from the Marine Hotel where the Englishmen stay...." His mother never worked at the Marine Hotel. But the vision of seven heads and ten feet, crippled him and he drew closer to the same girl who had taken him into the corn, to feel her comfort, to be protected from these beasts of the land, and to feel her breasts. "Wait!" she said, in an embarrassingly high voice, a stranger now to his advances, "who you think I is, boy? Who you think you feeling-up boy?" She pushed him aside, and he was spared greater embarrassment in that cool darkness where he could not see even his own feet in the thickness, and no one could see his furtive trembling hand, similar to the hand of Jane, disappearing from the side of the rails going back into the dense green corn. It was fifteen years after that rebuke before he had the strength to raise his hand from his side to touch a woman on her waist. And he saw the horse his mother was talking about, and which had ten heads, and forty feets; and he was in a road by himself, and the horse was coming in his direction and the eighty crescents of iron in its cantering madness were like the fright in a dream of standing in the middle of a tunnel with lights at the side, overhead, and curving in the short noisy distance round an invisible bend and hearing the loud clatter of an approaching train but not being able to decide which end of the tunnel is the entry or the exit, and then in his confusion all goes black, and only the noise now closer to a roar, brings him to resignation and the making of the sign of the Cross, two times on his shaking breast. Just before Jane had disappeared out of the rectangular train window, the man had seen her make a sign, and now that he had vomited that part of his past, he realizes that it was a Cross she was tracing in her broken ambition to hitch a ride to a big city where she thought her rags would be replaced by silk and stockings and pumps.

And he is in a dream, rumbled to sleep by the level of the sliding rails, by the lulling movement of the speed. He can hear his dream and he can hear the train. His head hits against the cold plate glass window, not hard enough to wake him, but strong enough to pierce the dream with the reality of knowing he is not dead, that he is disappearing from the small town, and without watching or counting the miles in the darkness outside, he sits like a man drugged from gin waiting for this journey to end. Jane passes through his dream one more time. She is wearing silk and black pantihose that is ribbed with an almost invisible design. And she has pumps on her feet. Her legs are strong from all the running she has done. Her breasts are prominent in a style and fashion of dignity and determination. His mother would have told her, "You walking like a woman now. With your chest push-out. If you have it, show it off, girl. Show it off." She is walking beside Jim. Not that the two of them are a couple. There is not that kind of love between them. She is walking beside Jim, because she could not get rid of him, her encumbrance, her disappointment, her hindrance, from catching that train that would have brought her sooner to glory and to the freedom she was seeking. Jane is in a dress that tells him she is a working woman, a woman who rises at five to make food for her children, two from Jim in the five years of her new life in the big city, and in that time, two years more than the contended legal space of decentness and trial and error to make her into spouse, woman, wife; and to make up his mind; Jim walks beside her as if he is not tied to her; as if he was plunked there by masculine ego; and not as her partner. He is dressed in a very expensive suit of shiny silk material. The bottoms of his trousers are narrow, and the "play" in the legs gives them a zoot-suit look. He has a long chain from his fob pocket hanging in a sweep by his knees and up again into his left trousers pocket. It looks like gold. The waist of the jacket is small and it shows the rippling muscles of his back that had chopped wood in the plantation year. The shoulders are flat and broad. And the jacket hangs like the flair in the skirt of the dress Jane is wearing. "Why're you always walking beside me dressed like a pimp? Am I picking fares for you? You'se my pimp? Or my *man*? The man I want walking beside me is a man dressed in overalls, and open-necked shirt in summer, a heavy sweater in winter, and boots reinforced with steel. A laboring man. A working man. A man who works. A man who knows sweat and who carries a lunch pail to the site." Jim has not worked since he arrived in the big city. "What do I want with a man walking beside me carrying a purse in his hand like if he is some *faggot!* And with a beeper like if he is some, some, some *pimp!* Or crack dealer! Or time-keeper. Who're you keeping time for?"

"Bitch."

It was as if he was fighting to catch his breath, so bitter and short and fierce was the way he uttered the word. It was a new word. It was a word he had heard her called by, years ago in the large plantation yard, swept so clean by him when he was a boy, and drenched in the life-giving sun, when his knowledge of the new language he was growing up with, English, was sufficient for him to ape the word *bitch*, spewed out of the mouth of the Master of the Slaves.

The towns and hamlets are fireflies in the darkness that surround the train as he moves in the snoring silence, coming into view, and before he can surmise where he is passing, and even after the trainman announces the place, it is gone. Like the dream of Jane and Jim. He wonders if they caught another train. But it could not be: this was the last train. The last train from the small town the short distance of a bridge spanning water that no longer moved. He can sense the smell of destination: the air is heavier; the cigarette smoke in the coach is thicker. The fireflies change into the eyes of cats in the darkness that is not so thick. Around him now, are lights as numerous as Christmas, but in the moving distance, all the same colour, against the black trunks of roads and intersections.

The woman in the small town becomes lovable the farther he is from her. Her dog is no longer a pest, but a pet that he could, with some understanding, cuddle and kiss, if he had three rums in his system to give him the strength and stomach. The small economizing room was as spacious as the coach, and the toilet with its sides made of tin, did not reverberate to the noise of his peeing as the shaking latrine on the train did, spewing his urine on the seat and making it difficult for him to aim in the unsteady bullseye of the soiled oval. The lights in the coach go out, just as the trainman announces the last town before his destination. And in that temporary darkness he forgets dog and woman, room and enclosed bathroom. He is standing, pushing papers into his leather bag, putting on his shoes, taking a last drag on the cigarette, checking that his Walkman is not left for a dishonest passenger to find and keep, getting into shape to manage the rush from the train and into the subway, and bounce women with large bags out of his way, and ignore the begging man, hungry at this time of night, as he can spare the time it takes to dig into his pocket less than he can spare the change.

All he is thinking of now is how short is the time to get from this train and the hissing steam down the stairs to the subway off the subway four stops north, and into his house to pour himself a stiff gin and tonic and listen to the midnight program of contemporary jazz. Before he leaves the train, stepping on the rickety iron step; "Watch your step, now," the same entreaty as "Spare any change?" and he has already wiped woman and dog, Jane and Jim out of his mind. He is back again in the big city. And it was only a train ride.

IN AN ELEVATOR

It was mid-November and after five o'clock, and most of the staff had left. It was snowing. And the evening, early as it was, looked like midnight. Hundreds of men and women had already streamed out from the building heading for the trains to the suburbs, and except for one woman who was in the ladies' room, almost the only people in the twenty-nine storeyed building of glass and steel were the heavily built Portuguese and Greek women who cleaned the offices and the washrooms.

The occupant in the ladies' room was Susan Cole. Tainted sea-food eaten at a place on the lake, the Fish Tackle & Bone Café, had given her a touch of diarrhea all day. It had magnified itself into a constant run to the bathroom. She waited in slight pain and with great embarrassment in the locked cubicle, while other ladies entered, chatted and gossiped while doing their business, and left.

Susan was a careful woman. She was tidy. She dressed well. Perhaps, above her means and salary. But the job was temporary: she was heading for Osgoode Hall Law School. She lived at home with her parents. Her father had been in hospital from June until two weeks ago, lying in silent writhing misery from his back which he had "put out" from playing old timers' hockey, after his wife had told him not to skate at his age, and he went and did and "put it out." She loved her father.

Susan was sensitive. Not only to the dirty language some of the women used in the ladies' washroom, and to the corny, horny jokes of the supervisory male staff, but also to the changing face of the city, and to the fabric of her own office: faces and accents. She was above all, sensitive to smells. On the subway, at a quarter to eight each morning, she traveled from home to office and had to stand for the thirty-one minutes of the journey because the train was jammed. She would be very close to men and women from lands she had not even come across in geography books at school. And she would smell and become aware of their lotions, their after-shave and the hair-sprays.

Earlier this afternoon, the chief executive officer had called her into his office, and had dictated a letter of such length and questionable syntax, that she cringed in her seat, sucked on her breath, gritted her teeth, and spent most of the dictating time looking through the window into the foreboding grey sky that hung over the Lake. Her stomach was grumbling. The curtain of bad weather was hanging round her like a mood, and she could barely make out her club, The Royal Canadian Yacht Club. But the sky began to clear. And the name of the restaurant she had eaten at came through the clouds, and the sight brought her lunch close to her mouth and lips. Half an hour before, she had vomited in the ladies' room. Now, she placed a man-sized white Kleenex to her red lips and missed a very technical phrase in the CEO's dictation. She closed her eyes. When she opened them, the nausea had passed. Clouds hid the name of the restaurant. And the dictation was at its conclusion. For a moment she could not move. But she had to think of the missing phrase. She was capable. Very intelligent. And inventive. And very uncomfortable.

She had rushed to the ladies' room the moment her boss got up from his deep-seated leather chair, and she sat on the cold porcelain bowl and was about to surrender to the turmoil in her stomach, when Grace entered with Joyce, carrying on a conversation. Susan raised her shoes, for she wore shoes that were distinctive in style, in colour and in quality, and she was known throughout the office as Shoes.

This afternoon, the two of them did not talk in whispers as they were sure they were alone.

"From ten this morning, she started. I counted three times before lunch."

"Didn't you tell me last Christmas, that she's engaged?"

"Me?"

"You said she's engaged."

"Not me."

"Must've been Anne, then."

"Couldn't have been!"

"Anne and her were reading about the man who molested the woman in the elevator last Friday."

"You think she's pregnant?"

"Could be."

"It happened at seven o'clock. It wasn't even midnight. At *seven*, imagine!"

"And in an insurance company building."

"Look! See my whistle? I don't leave home without it. But I wish I didn't have to catch the five-thirty so I could go with you to those classes."

"Last night, they taught us how to over-power a man with pepper spray."

"The papers said she was in the elevator with the man for four floors. Did you say pepper-spray?"

In all this time, with her shoes raised, out of sight, adding a tightness to her stomach muscles, and trying to control the rage within her bowels, Susan remained quiet and in great discomfort, barely hearing and unable to pay attention. But then she lost control. The toilet bowl erupted, and she hoped that the smell was not equal to the echo.

"Somebody!" Joyce exclaimed.

"I have to catch the five-thirty!"

"Have a good weekend."

"What're you doing this weekend? God, I have eight minutes!"

"This pepper-spray thing. You have seven and a half minutes...."

Susan was grateful when they'd gone. And she settled on the toilet seat, and tried to think of the cause. "It's the oysters!" She spoke it loud enough for the person who had entered after Grace and Joyce had left, to hear, and know that the bathroom was occupied at this late hour.

"Some person?" the cleaning lady asked.

There was silence, and then the noise from the locked cubicle.

"Some person?"

The cleaning lady retreated and closed the door; and parked her trolley and walked to the end of the corridor, where another cleaning woman inside the men's room was mopping the floor, with its door held ajar. They stood talking, waiting like watchmen for Susan to come out.

When Susan got up from the bowl, she could hardly stand, she was so weak. And when she walked to the wash basin, her high-heeled shoes clipped over the tiles, with less noise. Susan Cole was twenty-eight. And she had learned to walk this way, making noise with her heels, even when, at Bishop Strachan School for Girls, her shoes were Oxfords with half-inch rubber heels. At Bishop Strachan she'd been captain of the field hockey team, captain of the wrestling team, captain of the junior track and field team and ended up as Head Girl.

Grace and Joyce were convinced she looked down on them. They had attended a collegiate institute to boys *and* girls of working class background from Leaside. Once, Susan left a copy of the Bishop Strachan Alumni magazine on their desks. The two of them felt it was done to remind them of their place. In fact, Susan had left the magazine mostly to show them what she looked like at age ten.

Susan was not married; and they wanted to be able to say that in spite of her clothes from Holt Renfrew, and her Bishop Strachan schooling, her red shoes of leather and suede, she would find herself in precisely the predicament both of them had known. Grace was a single parent. And Joyce barely escaped that state through an abortion, suggested by her mother. So it was a digestible piece of gossip when they hoped that Miss Susan Cole would find herself in a state of want, rejection and dislocation they themselves had known.

Susan went back to her desk. It was now ten minutes past six. A woman in a blue uniform, came along the corridor with a trolley that was silent as an expensive European car. The woman held a dusting mop in her left hand, and humming under her breath, absent-mindedly, she passed it over the tubular pencil and ball-point holders, over the man-sized boxes of Kleenex, over the framed photograph of Susan's sweet-hearting man. This cleaning woman was once in a school of dress designers in Athens. She liked clothes and designs. Her first three years in this city, were spent bending over a power sewing machine, putting buttons on women's blouses in the garment district on Spadina Avenue; and sometimes falling asleep. She watched and waited and cursed her husband a little for being too slow in pulling himself up by the laces of his construction boots. She knew that if she got the chance, in two years she could make a woman of herself; and a man of her husband. And be successful like this woman, sitting at her desk, whom she would watch closely and love from a distance. Susan hated her.

Each morning, standing in the subway train, one of the hundreds of jostled women thrown against people from places like the one the cleaning woman came from, with her breasts and waist pressed against those men and those women who stared at her with lust and love and envy, all she could smell during those short minutes of the long ride was the aroma of garlic. And once, in an honest confession of her allergic reaction to it, she mentioned it to Joyce, not remembering that Joyce was Joyce Maviglia before she became Joyce McCarthy, before she became divorced.

Now after all this time, she got it. It was the garlic she had eaten at Fish, Tackle & Bone Café. But the garlic had been buried in the fresh shrimps large as little lobsters. She sniffed the air now. The woman with the silent trolley went about her cleaning humming under her breath. Susan knew she smelled garlic.

Returning from lunch on Wednesday, in the brilliant life-giving afternoon, and taking a last puff on her Players Light, Susan moved without paying attention to the elevator whose arrow was green and pointing upwards. She wanted the twentieth floor. The elevator she got into went only to the fourteenth. In she went, and did not press a number. Before the door closed, a black man stepped forward, barely missing the aimed palm of the door, intent it seemed, on cutting his body into half. He smiled at her. Susan did not smile. He smiled again, and said, "Jesus Christ!" The door missed him. He smiled again.

It was warm inside the elevator. A voice in the mechanism said, "Going up." Music started to play in the middle of a song. She did not recognize the song. The elevator was moving. The black man had not yet pressed a number. She noticed this, and wondered. The elevator became very uncomfortable. Susan passed her left hand, with the ring on her little finger, across her neck. On the ring was the crest of Bishop Strachan. Her hand remained on her neck for a longer time than she would take to remove a thread from her collar. Danger came into her stomach, like the first signs of diarrhea.

This man was thinking of the interview he was going to; that he was late. He tightened his tie, slackened the knot, and tightened it again. He looked at the piece of paper in his right hand, realized something was wrong, and when the elevator stopped and the door opened, he knew he had taken the wrong lift.

Back at her desk, that afternoon, she'd accused herself for having *those* feelings; and she searched in her past and went back over her days at Bishop Strachan: Amantha was from Barbados, wasn't she? Yes, I remember her accent. And she was good in class, especially in Latin and she was in my House and played field hockey better than me, better than anybody else, and the time I knocked her down, did I knock her down because she was challenging me, because she was smaller, because she was Amantha? Or? And that other one from the Bahamas who thought she was the cat's meow better than any of us, the best of us with her father the prime minister; and getting her parcels special delivery and couriered to her; and that time when I told Miss Sweeney that is was *her*, she was the culprit who had written the dirty word on the blackboard about Miss Sweeney: *lesbian*, and she traveled over every remembered detail of those years of childhood and of pleasure as they were meant to be, without bias but with the perspiring competitiveness of bright, privileged young girls. "Could I have offended any of them?"

She was tugged from these reveries and confessions by the ringing of the telephone on her desk.

"I'm seeing that bastard again." It was her father. "The bones-doctor." His voice revived her. "Drinks after work?" That put an end to her acrimonious sadness.

So, on this evening, two days later, she began to fix her face in the silver compact she had bought at Chanel on Bloor Street, pursing her lips, drawing them up into a thin line, making them into the shape she used to kiss the man who used lubricated condoms with her; drawing them to one side, the right, as if she had undergone surgery for a disfigured face; and then she did the same thing, drawing her lips to the left.

She removed a speck from the corner of her left lid, checked that her eyes were clean, and then applied mascara. The lipstick was red, full-bodied and strong. She tilted her bottle of Chanel Number 17, and placed the finger with the invisible drop on her left wrist, and with that wrist rubbed her right wrist. And then she passed the bottle under her nostrils, and rested it lightly against her neck.

In the oval looking glass in the compact, she caught the cleaning woman's eyes. They were in full focus watching her, studying her. She became agitated. She went back over that time when the word was written on the blackboard. *Lesbian.*

The woman was standing in front of the trolley, and she seemed to be imitating Susan's motions, her left hand raised as if it was holding some small object; and her right hand reproducing the touching of nostrils, neck and wrists. Susan kept her full in the centre of the looking glass. She could see her eyes, the colour of her cheeks, and the mole at the corner of her mouth, on the right side. The cleaning woman's eyes were green.

Nervously, Susan examined her own eyes, going over the make-up, and snapped the compact shut, intending by that action to shut the prying green eyes out and obliterate that dirty word written years ago on the blackboard.

She breathed on her fingernails, at the red nail polish on her manicured hands; passed her hand while still sitting on the leather chair with the protecting cushion for pack pains, over her well-shaped and endowed hips. She glanced at her legs and promised, that in spite of the pain, she would have to do something about her veins. The veins that were beginning to crawl in irregular blue rivulets beneath her light-grey pantihose: have to take time off, have to check my health benefits, have to tell them about the hospital and co-ordinate with the surgeon, have to tell Mother and Father, have to put my desk in order and have to give my tickets to

Joyce or Grace.... Anne...? Someone who'd appreciate ballet and, "Oh, my God! Look at the time!"

And she rose from her chair, put her purse into her bag strapped over her right shoulder, and walked out with her heels reverberating against the tiles, noisier now that the entire floor was empty.

Smoking was not allowed on her floor, but she took the box of Players Light from her purse, placed a cigarette into her mouth and then removed it. The red smear from her lips stained the tip; and then she put the cigarette back into her mouth, and fished for the box of wooden matches in her large black shoulder bag made of imitation crocodile skin. The grey-green small box with two capital P's written back-to-back on it, she held in her hand, until the elevator came to her floor. She got inside.

She was about to press G, when she noticed that every single floor button, from 20 to G, had been pressed and illuminated, even that for the basement. She lit the cigarette, filling her lungs with the first deep pull, and kept the smoke there for a long moment, and exhaled and relaxed and felt the weight of the day and the annoyance with the diarrhea dissipate, and thank God it was over; and the cleaning woman looking at her in that way, as if she was about to ask her a question; but, "What the hell did she want?"

And then the door closed and she endured the slight nausea of her stomach falling as the elevator started to descend; and then the smoother sailing down the shaft in the enclosed, paneled cage. Alone to enjoy her cigarette, alone to travel down the twenty floors, along to smoke her prohibited cigarette, alone and with some sense of regaining strength after love. She thought of the man. And only after enjoying the expectation of this privacy that she knew was going to last only until someone else got into the elevator, "The building is empty," did it really sink in and become anxiety, that each of the twenty illuminated circles representing the twenty floors would first have to be obliterated, that the cage would stop at each circle before they all could be wiped out, before she could reach the ground.

The first stop was sudden. She looked out at plants on a receptionist's desk, and compared the office displayed before her with her own, and decided that hers was a more prestigious place to work. When the door was about to close, a man in a blue uniform with his name written on it, came into view hauling a long fat rubber connection; and just as the door closed, she heard the hum of a vacuum cleaner. She was becoming irritable. "Why would that bitch do this to me?"

She looked at her watch. It was seven. She had no dinner appointment, no places to go, but she still continued looking at her watch.

She was on the nineteenth floor. The elevator was descending to the eighteenth and she was now between floors. They say that during the power failure in New York City, men and women were caught in elevators between floors for hours together, and when they came out, some of them were pregnant. And she looked at the button marked *emergency*, and she glanced at the telephone behind its glass protection; and she wondered how long it takes for someone, police, superintendent, repairman, ambulance attendant to arrive? And how would they arrive! Do they come through the top of the elevator?

The eighteenth floor. A man steps into the elevator. He is wearing sneakers. The laces are not tied. They are the kind that basketball stars use for making shots slam-bang, and defying gravity. They are white with red and blue slashes; and she cannot make out the name of their manufacturer. The trousers are black jeans, down over the tip of the sneakers which look like boots, they are high above the ankle; and the bagginess of the trousers causes her to wonder how tall this man is. She moves her eyes from his sneakers up his legs, his waist, and down again. She cannot bring herself to look into his face. Not yet. "He's taller than me!" And her eyes reach the bottom of his coat or windbreaker, and she can imagine how large the shoulders are, and can see the colours of red and green and yellow against the black background of the windbreaker. And then she sees the expanse of his chest and the thin yellow line of electrical cord joining the yellow Walkman's noise to his ears, going deaf. For she can hear the noise, even though she cannot follow the Rhythm. "Rap!" she says to herself. And in the slow descent, for she is now travelling with someone she does not want to be travelling with, the cigarette is still in her mouth, and she allows the ash to grow. And she stands in the middle of the small space shared with the in-truder in this cage, realizing that the man is facing her, and has not moved an inch since he violated her right to be safe and silent and alone in this elevator. For after all, she works here. And was here first.

And the elevator moves slower now, taking as much time to reach one floor below, as all the nineteen to travel, and in the death-like quiet, with nothing else to do, for she has already painted a picture of his attire, and could pick him out of any police line-up with her eyes closed, she goes over in her mind, with the tough cigarette in her mouth, with smoke and ash getting longer, word for word, her accusations of rape and assault. A kick in the crotch. A scream. Where is my goddamn whistle? Did I leave it on the desk when the goddamn cleaning woman was staring at me? My whistle is attached to my subway tokens holder. Press the button marked *emergency*, and scare the bastard? Do not give him the impression I am scared. Be aggressively defensive. Remember the lessons in karate. Wish I'd attended those classes Joyce goes to, with that pepper-spray thing! And look the son-of-a-bitch in his eye.

She raises her eyes. He is staring at her from behind tinted glasses. Disguise! And sees the earphones. And the baseball cap.

With a large white X. And turned backwards, so that she can see he has one of those haircuts popular with rappers. And thinking of music, she realizes with some shock that she has not heard music since he entered the cage. It was music already piping through the speakers above their heads. And it was not even Rap.

And the man, in panic, standing before her, placed in this closeness against his will, watched her as she lit another cigarette, as she coughed, as something in her throat went up and down, as he saw her hand that held the cigarette, shaking.

Holy shit what am I gonna do stuck with this bitch in this elevator? If it wasn't for my Mom, I wouldn't be in this. Forcing me to take a part-time job. Dad said no; study hard and you will get to college. I'm studying hard, for college and now *this*. What with me and her in here, how the fuck now am I gonna explain I didn't do nothing that I am only delivering a parcel.

He's waiting for the seventh floor. Perhaps, the fifth, the fourth? He will stop the elevator between the eighth and seventh. That's why he's wearing dark glasses. Why else would he be wearing dark glasses in an elevator, seven o'clock at night? I see them on television wearing dark glasses. I see them all the time in the news, in dark glasses.

Boy, am I gonna be glad when this reaches the ground floor. Holy shit am I glad I have this Walkman in my ears! And I was gonna put it in my pocket before I entered this building, I wonder if she could know that I ain't listening to nothing, since this stopped working. Batteries dead. So, it's only style and to prevent people from staring at me like it keeps me invisible. I wonder what this chick is thinking? She sure smokes like all those white girls in my grade thirteen class. Like Jane. Now, if Jane and me were still dating.... Twenty a day? Shit!

And the elevator, passing through all this time in its slow journey, reached its destination sooner than either the man or the woman expected. In a strange way neither of them desired the end. And he could see her body relax as if she had just finished exercising and could now breathe easier. He saw her hand, no longer shaking, drop the cigarette on the floor of the elevator, and how she crushed it with the tip of her high-heeled shoe. She grounded it into the carpet until it turned to brown flour. They were red suede shoes. And he said to himself, "The last time. Never again."

The area of the lobby was bright. He could see the winter light reflecting on the tall sheets of glass and metal in the building across the street. Outside, there were people walking. They looked happy and secure. Would they know, or care that he had just come through a baptism of fear and of violence which could have been done to him because of that fear? And what might he have done to her?

She pushed past him. He stood at the front of the cage, allowing her to pass. She looked to see if the night security guard was behind the counter. This counter with its lights and buttons and controls and monitors looked like the controls in an airplane. It made the guard and the job he did, more important than it really was. She too could see women walking in the street. Some of them were alone. Two women were standing up, chatting and laughing; and all of them oblivious to her experience with this ass-hole, from twenty floors above their heads right down to this saving, thank God, protected lobby, because I was here first, and I work here, and no goddam immigrant or cleaning woman or black son-of-a-bitch, nobody's gonna make me feel threatened and live like a victim in my own fucking country, province....in my city.

Now, did Cecil lock the doors before he went on his coffee break?

The man was beside her. And he too wondered if they were about to face another hindrance. But holy shit, at least people outside on the street can see me and her, and I can tell my side of the story, and they gotta believe my innocence.

She knew she could pick him out *like that* from any lineup in a police station, even if he left his dark glasses at home to hide the fact. And she knew that never again, not ever, would she be found *dead* in an elevator with a black man. She'd get off first! And wait until a white man came in! Or remain standing in front of the elevator, even if it took till time for work the next day! I can pick him out *like that*, in any lineup. But why didn't I get off at the very next floor after he entered? Why? Why?

The door onto Yonge Street was unlocked. He had used too much force, anticipating the hindrance, and so when he pushed the door outwards, he almost lost his balance. But he smiled. And turned and looked her in the face, and smiled once more. And he said, "Lady?" She was surprised to hear his voice. His hand was on the polished horizontal bar, holding his half of the glass door open, allowing her to precede him. He had forgotten his ordeal in the cage locked up with her. She did not say thanks for opening the door. She walked out as he held the door.

Before she reached the edge of the sidewalk, she had the white cigarette pack of Players Light in her left hand, and the matches with the two Ps on the box, in her right: "I'm *safe* here!" Her purse and handbag were on the cold cement of the sidewalk between her feet. He turned to her and said, "Lady, so much smoking not good for you. Says so on the box."

She looked at him with no change of expression. Her expression before he had spoken was relief, of victory mixed with a tinge of anger at having been helpless and without inventiveness to control the terror of his company. She placed the cigarette back into the box. She dropped the matches into the large black imitation crocodile shoulder bag. She took the bag and the purse from the cold pavement. She wanted to see in which direction he was going to turn. And then she stood and watched his jumping strides, as if he was a basketball star or a ballet dancer, moving as if he was walking on air. The unbuttoned multi-coloured broad-shouldered jacket blowing in the wind, made him look like a bird, free and dancing in his stride to the inner music pouring through his ears.

Her face felt warm and flushed. Her hands began to feel the weight of the purse and handbag. But she was accustomed to this every day on the packed subway train. This new weight however, made her feel her body and the blood in her cheeks and the slight pain in the veins in her legs. But more than that, she could feel something like excitement, like new life in her body, a kind of transfusion changing her blood to desire.

And he was disappearing fast from her, going in the direction of the lake, and the Fish, Tackle & Bone Café, towards Harbourfront. Were they having a concert, or a poetry reading tonight at Harbourfront? And even when tears began to wash her face and cloud her eyes and vision and made it impossible for her to identify him in the distance, she blamed the cold air that now brought the tears. She knew she would still remember the white sneakers with their slashes of blue and red; and the baggy trousers that fell over the top of the sneakers that looked like boots, above the ankle. And he was tall and his head was shaven in the new style; and she could see the large white X, and the yellow cord to his ears.

BEGGARS

There is a bank machine at the top of the subway stairs. A wind comes up from the subway. In winter the wind is strong and cold. The winter has dragged on until early May, and this morning, as I move away from the line at the bank machine, I am brushed by a woman who carries a soft leather briefcase in her left hand, a large handbag in her right, struggling against the stream of people and cursing as she tries to stuff her cash into her red purse. There is a gold-painted snap on her purse. I hold five twenties from the machine and I am trying to put them into my wallet as I go through the heavy glass doors to the subway.

Once inside, I face a new stream of men and women, mostly women. And the man. He stands in the tiled corner, no more than five feet from me, staring me in the eye, and then, he drops his eyes suddenly to my hand, and is counting the bills I hold, five winks of calculations.

"Spare any change?"

His manner is not pleading. And is not condescending. It is like a command. I ignore his outstretched hand.

"Fuck you!"

It is loud enough for me to hear.

I am absorbed by the large woman coming full at me. I feel she is about to smash me into the cold hard tiled wall. In her left hand is a yellow Walkman. Her eyes are focused on the pounding drums of metal that seep through the earphones. She does not smile, nor dance in her walking, to the music in her ears. And she does not see me.

The man in the corner is looking at my hand. I am pushed to one side, his side, by the weight of the woman.

"Sorry," I say.

"Fuck you!" she says.

The man is putting out his hand, a manicured hand, to her, and she drops him a coin.

"Thanks," he says. In the next breath, "Spare any change?" reaching into the flow of people. The woman has melted into the crowd.

I put the five twenties in my wallet, take the green ticket the size of a stamp from the ticket seller, and calculate the amount of cash I carry, none of which is for overdue bills, or buying lunch, or buying books, or buying anything. I do not need any of this cash; there is no emergency; and I wonder if the man....

The subway platform is crowded. As I force myself in, I am pressed against a man on my left, and a woman on my right. I try to recall if my aftershave lotion was slapped on my face too generously, and I pass over in my mind each detail of my dressing and washing: deodorant, toothpaste and mouth-wash; and is there grease on the knot of my silk tie? Is the button on my shirt, just over my belly-button undone? As I am retracing these absurdities and insecurities, the train stops. I am jerked against the warmth of the woman, I can feel her stomach, and her breasts, and her legs which touch mine; and I feel I am in the sea and that her blood, which I tell myself I can feel, is warm invigorating salt water. She is holding on to me, for balance.

"Sorry," she says.

"Sorry," I say.

But I am not sorry. She squeezes her eyes shut. Opens them, in an expression of friendship and forgiveness. I am still pressed against her stomach and her breasts, and the silk of her pantihose, or it could be the natural softness of her legs, like the Albolene Cream I apply to my legs and the soles of my feet after my bath. She closes her eyes again.

Her eyes remain closed. And I try to put her back, a half hour, or an hour-and-a-half, back into her house, where everything she touches, and does not touch, is as personal as the body cream she applies after her hurried shower. Does she know of Albolene Cream? They say it was invented for black bodies only.

I see her body stiffen as she wakes in bed, stretching her legs; and the cotton nightgown, which has no shape to reveal her waist and breasts, is riding up along one leg, above her thigh; from tossing in the nightmare that visited her and that rode her most of the night.

Her mortgage is up for renewal. Her husband is out of work. And has not worked since Christmas. He drove his car to Oakville for eighteen years to assemble cars; and yesterday he drove all that distance back to Scarborough in angry silence, and did not mention the meeting he'd had with their bank manager. He is an unemployed man, with no security to put against a loan.

She is taking over the pants in her home, is turning into a man, is managing all the things around the house. He is snoring still, on the left hand side of the queen-sized bed, settled and unmoving as if he were sleeping off a double-shift on the assembly line. She does not like the contentment on his face, or the sound of his breath pouring through his mouth.

I can see her stretching her legs to their full length, and see her pass her left hand across her eyes. Light is already in their bedroom. She pulls her nightdress down to cover her nakedness, although his eyes are closed, and he is still snoring. I see her sit upright, with effort. She glances at the deadened man beside her. She glances at the red eyes of the alarm clock which did not alarm this morning. "Oh my God!" It is shock. Exasperation. Defeat. It is the hour. She has to see the bank manager today during her forty-five minute lunchtime.

She walks into the bathroom. It is decorated pink, including the cake of Swan soap she bought at Shoppers Drug Mart during her forty-five minutes yesterday. And the velour on the cover of the toilet bowl is pink and so is the one on the water tank. Her toothbrush is pink. I hear the water running for her shower and she tests the heat, squeezing at the same time the green toothpaste from the middle of the pink tube, and then she drops the nightgown from her neck and shoulders, probing her breast just in case, and promises to visit her doctor. The nightgown falls to the ground, to the fluffy scatter-mat. The mat is pink. After her shower, still naked and wet, she wipes her face, and applies her make-up. No emergency can make her hasten this ritual.

I have put her at forty years of age. Perhaps, thirty-nine. She is tall. About five feet, seven. And well-built. Her hair is brownish-red. And it reaches the middle of her neck. Her skin is smooth and not white although she is white. It looks as if she has returned from the south, perhaps three weeks ago. Her tan is just disappearing. She knows she is attractive. I can see her walking with this confidence, with the heavy fall of her feet as if she is two hundred pounds. She is one hundred and twenty. But I know that some women walk with greater ponderance than their weight suggests. I see her moving from the warmed bathroom, and for a moment I cannot see her face clearly in the mirror because of the steam in the room; and she goes into the kitchen, and pours herself a cup of coffee, made automatically. She places the mug on the shining counter top, and goes to the fridge to get a tumbler of fresh orange juice. She goes back into the bedroom.

Her husband is now on his back. He has slipped over to her side of the bed. She imagines that someone she cannot see is holding his nostrils tight, only releasing them at the last moment, so that he seems on the point of suffocating. Once, in her daily anger and irritation with her job and her husband, the thought passed through her mind. Suffocation. And it lingered there. And once, she drove with him to Niagara Falls and saw the whales playing in a tranquil pool, just as her own two children played when they were still young enough to frolic in the bathtub with plastic ducks and plastic bears. She wonders now, as she looks down with distaste at her husband, so close to death, if she has a mind for it; and she wonders now, suffering her own suffocation, why she never gave her children a dolphin made of plastic. Or a whale. Or a fish.

She pulls out the top drawer on her side of the bureau of ten drawers, five on each side, and takes out her underwear. And rips the plastic package from the pantihose, and drops the hose. They land on her husband's face. He continues breathing. "When?" she says. "When?"

I see her choose red panties. They are silken. Her bra is red and silken. Her camisole is red. I see it is silk. She puts the pantihose on, and then the panties, and then her shoes, which look almost red. She opens the concertina-like door of the clothes cupboard, wondering why she didn't set out this morning's outfit last night, after her bath in pink bubbles. She puts the dress on, and runs her hands over her hips, and she smooths the rich material which covers her luscious body for a moment from my eyes. She turns in the long mirror built into the door, and smiles, and leaves and goes back into the kitchen, seeing the glass of orange juice and the mug of black coffee, both cold, and turns on the radio with the red eyes, and listens to the report of roads and traffic and accidents *". . . and the Don Valley is clogged up. Police report three accidents in the south-bound lanes. If you have to take the Don Valley Parkway, give your-self...."*

The eyes of the clock say eight. She sips the cold coffee, rests the mug on the counter, and then she takes a sip of orange juice.

I see her husband move in his sleep, and reach out a hand that crawls up under her dress, raising the skirt. He pulls her against the bed and forces his naked body against her silk dress, and I see her protesting and pleading, "I can't! I can't!" and he pleads too, and as usual he has his way.

Her face reflects that short, passionate, hurtful moment. She lowers the car window and the cold wind comes in and kisses her face and the tears on her cheeks. He is silent behind the wheel, beside her. He is thinking neither of work, nor of the pleasure he has just had. He is driving her to the subway station, "As part of the deal."

And now, I see her standing beside me. My eyes open and she stands against me with her eyes closed and with a smile lingering on her face. Her lowered eyelids remind me of the dream she is now completing, the dream that tormented her through the night in that house in the suburbs. Her blouse is pink in the bad light of the subway train. And her skirt is, to my eyes that do not know colours, the colour of a rose.

The train jerks, coming to a stop. It is the first stop since I have made this woman's acquaintance. The stop is sudden. It causes her to open her eyes. I can see something more than friendliness in her eyes. What I see is something like disgust. The train had come to a stop as if the driver, taking us through darkness, had forgotten to count the red station light markers. She looks like a woman who has missed her station. But she does not move. There is no space for her to move in. And I am thankful, and blessed by the touching of her flesh against my legs, the benediction of her flesh, and I wonder if she is aware of this. I am thankful, pressed against her living, breathing body.

Perhaps she is a woman too scared by this uninvited closeness to protest the assault my body causes her. Perhaps she does not understand the rawness of the pressure against her thighs. Perhaps, she is not aware of her pressure against my thighs.

And then, like a woman in a sleep that is not deep, she starts, tosses long strands of reddish brown hair out of her eyes, as she would coming out of the sea, and is immediately, immaculately, a different woman.

Her body strikes mine. The train is hot and uncomfortable. I smell her anxiety as she pushes past me, a perfume I know. I can also smell my underarm deodorant.

She is taken back, back for half an hour, or an hour-and-a-half, in her own mind, before she was flattened against the door which closed and held her there unmoving, hardly breathing. When she woke this morning, the first thing she smelled was a damp sourness, and the first thing she saw was a small cockroach crawling away from her face as she lay half-asleep on the double mattress on the hardwood floor. She closed her eyes in disgust. She knew she had to kill the bastard. She reached for the box of Kleenex, intending to fold a tissue into four and measure the distance and the amount of force she was going to use to crush it on the white bed sheet.

She moved slowly, silently, stealthily. The cockroach was watching her. Cockroaches, she'd learned after two days in this apartment are sneaky bastards. They are evil. They prefer darkness to light. And she always remembered her mother telling her, from when she was seven years old, never trust a son-of-a-bitch who can't come out in the open, he's nothing but a fucking roach. It took her time to realize that her mother was not referring to marijuana or to the darting pest she'd seen only once in the basement flat she'd shared with the man she'd wedded ten years later. Her mother had been talking about the man she'd married.

Hardly moving, her breath held, she dug into the Kleenex box, searching the bottom of the box, realizing she had used them all the night before while sitting on this same mattress, on the single soiled sheet, wiping her eyes, watery from sadness, and from allergies. She watched the cockroach. It was watching her. Then it scurried in a small arc. She lifted herself onto her elbows. Her nightgown was gathered at her waist. She was restricted. She held her left hand over the cockroach. It was sitting motionless, as if in a trance. Her left hand! Since she was small she had done all the things that disgusted her with her left hand. She used her left hand to take cough syrup from the ugly brown bottle. She used her left hand to open the Bible in Sunday school every Sunday morning for the first ten years of her life. It was her left hand in which she held the engagement ring of the man she married. It was her left hand that had taken it off. She had caressed his thighs with her left hand. Now this killing had to be carried out with her left hand. It did not move. She brought the hand down, and the mattress gave a dull sound, the sound of the body of the man she had married as he slumped and fell back asleep, the man she had broken up with four days before. When she turned her hand over, her palm bore only a black stain, a fountain pen stain. Before going to bed, she'd written a letter to a friend to ask for a place to stay.

The cockroach disappeared. It was past seven. She thought of preparing for work, a shower, dressing, make-up, a cup of coffee; but black without sugar. She saw black scurrying roaches, some more brown than black, motherfuckers, pregnant, or gluttons over spilled sugar and the enticing grease round the dirty stove elements.

She ran to the dark bathroom, and her stomach, never strong, never tough, erupted. The sink was rusty near the plughole. There was no chain, no stopper. When she opened the cold water tap, just before the water came, three cockroaches ran up the side of the sink, and crawled on her nightgown. She started to cry. She had not turned the bathroom light on, and when she did turn it on, the dingy walls of the bathroom were alive with moving dots. She broke down and cried. The only word that passed her lips was, "When."

"When I was seventeen, when I was seventeen, I was still so...." She had blonde stringy hair, a girl from a poor family; and she sat with her father and mother every Saturday night round the large table in the kitchen, covered with an oil-skin cloth and the shells from peanuts, and they sang songs and hymns from the book they had given her in Sunday school; and the moment she finished grade nine, and was looking forward to going farther, her mother died, and her father left home one morning when the snow was up to his knees, and he did not find his way back. After seven days, she and the four little ones gave up looking through the window.

"When I was seventeen, I was still so young, I met Rick...." Rick was handsome and wore his hair long, as long as hers. He would come around, clean, and always in his suede windbreaker, and shiny shoes in the latest style, pointed toes. Rick was something in those days. When she was late coming home from the restaurant where she worked as a waitress, after she gave up looking through the kitchen window, after she decided it wasn't worth a fuck wasting time looking for that bastard, their father, Rick would be sitting at the kitchen table amusing her brothers and sisters. He'd be all decked out, ready to take her to the Saturday night dance at the Catholic Centre. The Catholics had the best dances, and the best bingo games.

It was at a Friday night bingo game that Rick put his hand on her leg, rubbing his hand up and down her thigh. He was so good to the children whenever she was kept back at the restaurant by the manager. The manager had seen her grow from a grade nine girl into an orphan of sorts, into a blossoming girl with bursting breasts, always clean and tidy, who went to church every Sunday. He wanted to screw her. He was crude. That is what he said on the second night he pretended that he wanted to talk to her about her serving manner at the tables. "Bingo!" she screamed. Rick's hand fell. And her leg became cold. "Bingo." It was two hundred dollars.

They walked the three blocks home in the cold with snow up to their ankles. She was not wearing winter boots. She had promised herself a pair that Saturday in a store around the corner from the restaurant. Rick held her hand. He was nobody's fool. He had gone as far as grade twelve until his father died and then his mother had taken another man who treated him like a dog till he ran away, and had to serve a little time, in jail, not much, where he learned his trade. Cutting up animals in an abattoir. For Canada Packers. He could lift the split carcass of a cow all by himself. And that was also when he went into boxing, and lasted two amateur matches.

When she screamed "Bingo!" she was shaking. She was crying. She was happy. She remembered her father, wishing he had not left, for if he'd come back, and he'd been at home, she could have put every penny in his hand. She loved her father. She loved her father more than she loved her mother. And she loved Rick, too. When she shouted, the three hundred people, mostly women old enough to be her mother, erupted in cheers; strangers clapped their hands as if they were at her wedding reception, and her new bridegroom had just cut the cake with a knife and slipped cake into her mouth with his tongue, longer than the knife. She took the money from the woman. The woman said, "Congratulations."

She stood there, not knowing what to say. And the woman said, "Take it. Take it, child. It's yours. It's all yours. Spend it wisely." She bent her knees, not knowing why she should pay respect to a woman she did not know. It was her money, after all. But she curtsied, and when she returned to Rick's side, the expression on his face was one of pride. She remembered that. It was also envy. She remembered that too. Years later, all she could say was, "That son-of-a-bitch!"

He walked beside her. He lit a cigarette. He chucked it into the snow. She could hear the freight train that ran a little distance from her home, at all hours of the night. Sometimes, when she was having pain at that time of the month, she counted the cars from the bumping noise; sometimes, when she was sitting up with her youngest sister who had a cold, she heard the train rumbling through the neighbourhood and wondered how a train found its way in the darkness, without accident; sometimes, after they were married, when she was waiting for Rick to come home, she wished she could hear the train, that she was in one of the coaches, cabooses, whatever you called them, and that she was travelling all night; and sometimes, she charted its course, followed it, the moment she heard the horn as it emerged from somewhere in the West End and entered the area of Davenport, along Dupont, going east until it seemed it was in her own backyard on Dupont at Bathurst, then down, down past Avenue Road, through the swank district of Rosedale, and she wondered what those people thought of the noisy, rumbling train.

He held her hand and said he wished he had the money to get a Mustang from the dealer he knew. It was a fantastic chance, he said. A fantastic car. "We could take trips every weekend." All he needed was a small down payment. He passed the lot every day after work, he'd talked to the salesman, who promised him a deal. He said, "Just the two of us, me and you, we could go to Niagara

Falls, see how it runs on the highway, like a charm," and then they'd maybe go to New York.

He held her hand but she was thinking of her aunt on the mother's side who'd come down at Christmas and offered to take the children to Orillia. She'd miss them. She would be lonely without them. But she could have Rick for herself. And she would not have to wait until after midnight to make sure they were asleep, so she could do it on the couch with Rick. Once, almost reaching that time, she had closed her eyes, pulling expectation faster through her body, but something warned her about complete submission, and she had kept her eyes open, and out of the bedroom where they all slept on bunk-beds, out of the greater darkness of that small room, came her little sister, unsure where she was, rubbing her eyes, calling. She'd jumped up, forgetting she was undressed. She'd made the sign of the cross, and then had led the child back into the dark small room.

"What the fuck!" he'd said, as she searched in the darkness for her dress, found it on the floor, and put it back on; and sat on the couch beside him. Under her leg, she could feel a wetness. She felt shame. "What the fuck!"

When did I decide to marry that bastard? When did I throw my life away...sitting now on the mattress with her overnight bag beside her on the hardwood floor, the cockroaches crawling in and out of it; she counted ten little ones; and her shoes and pantihose in the bag; her alarm clock beside her on the left hand. And she smiled and wondered if there was something wrong with her that in all her life she always placed her alarm clock, the same alarm clock, as a young girl, as a married woman, and now as a woman alone, on the left side: she was right-handed.

It started when he was drunk. He always said he'd had a hard day at the meat packers, he blamed it on his work, and on the beers he had chugalugged before coming home; and then he walked out, angrier than before, and she spent the time sobbing and reading her small red leather Bible. Her mother's gift the day she was confirmed.

Every time he was drunk, he blamed work, all the cutting up of carcasses, and he blamed the beers he drank, and the chasers of rye whisky at the bar around the corner; and he walked out, after he'd delivered the blows to her body and face, any place his blind hands and fists could find, and she sat sobbing and thankful that there was no child to witness all this; and she continued to read her small red leather Bible, torn at the spine.

In the midst of her sobbing, she planned how she would leave him, and be safe so that he would not know where she lived, and follow her, and stand in the shadows, outside. She went to work on Monday mornings at the restaurant wearing dark glasses to hide the swelling around her eyes; and she hid the wemms on her face and neck with make-up.

When it happened the last time, four nights ago, he almost killed her. He slapped her around. And she did not put up her hands to shield the blows. She stood there, feeling the pain and the humiliation deep down. He was not satisfied. His anger was not effective, there was no painful reaction. So, he began to beat her with his fists. He was in the ring again, fighting his first amateur bout and the man in front of him was taking his best shots. He struck her with a right cross. And he remembered that it was the second round, and the man in front of him was dancing around, making him look clumsy and foolish before the screaming crowd. "Ya bum! Ya bum!" He could hear the boos now, five years later. And he hit her with a left hook. And there was silence. He could hear the silence around him, he could smell the ointment, and taste the blood that had formed in his mouth from the blows this stupid son-of-a-bitch, the fancy-foot-work dude had caused. Now, he could smell her perfume, and her body. And in the midst of his violence there was an urge to screw her, fuck her to death. The left hook had made her face ugly. And just before it landed, he could still see her beautiful face, so fresh and so beautiful, the face he had kissed so many times, the face he gloried in when they were out together in the neighbourhood tavern drinking beer. And when his hand left her face, it reached for her blouse, and even though he did not intend it, his hand ripped away most of her blouse. And he could see that she was not wearing a bra. It was unexpected. If he could call back the anger, the violence, the slaps and the blows, he would have caressed her breasts which had given him so much comfort and satisfaction.

He wished he could call back the violence.

She said nothing. A long time. A time in which she relived every day of her life. In which she saw herself dead. A time when nothing else existed but her small roped-off ring inhabited by blows and sounds and boos and punches and blood. She did not exist outside of this. He saw it too, and it made him mad. As if he had thrown his best punches, and the foe in front of him was absorbing all his toughness and meanness, all his power.

He grabbed her by the neck and squeezed. He was getting delight from the power of his hands. Her eyes became wider, and then were closed. Her colour was changing. She was beginning to shake and quiver. And become subject to his strength. And again the astonishing urge to make love *to* her, to screw her, to fuck her, mixed with his anger, making his action one of delight. A smile came to his face. She saw it. And if was then that she felt this was the last time. She saw death. And she saw the ring begin to get smaller, and the three ropes were getting closer to her, and were about to wrap themselves round her. And miraculously, the ring stopped its constricting, and began to expand back outwards. It became the room in which he was strangling her. It became as large as the house itself; larger, larger, until the entire neighbourhood was encompassed. And she could see life outside this arena of blows and insult and degradation.

She thought she had killed him. He crouched over, holding his testicles, bending over until he was like a hairpin, grabbing his testicles to quell the agonizing pain. She thought she had killed him. And that is how she left him, on his knees, moaning, clutching himself, with a look of helplessness in his eyes, which she saw turning to inexplicable love.

And this is what went through her mind as she lay helpless on the mattress in the borrowed, empty apartment, with cockroaches crowding around her. And this is what went through her mind as she stood, in the crowded subway car, pressed by the man who was trying to read her thoughts, who applied more force to her thigh, this stranger whose cologne or perfume or aftershave lotion was so much like the scent of Rick when she'd first met him, so much so she wished she could take a chance with him.

The train stops. She comes alive from the corridors of her past she had been walking during its ride, and the doors open, and she is bright in the fluorescent light of the platform, and as she nears the concrete steps she is moved a little faster by the crowd behind her, touching her, brushing her. She can already see the light of the day pouring down the exit, in the shaft of concrete, and she can feel the power of the sun and she sees a white cloud sailing in the skies, and it is this that pulls her from the underground rough walls of the exit, up into the concrete of the street.

I see her leave. And with her there leaves a part of myself, for I had fashioned and created her in the image of lust of my desire this morning when there was nothing else on my mind.

I try to remember the woman's clothes. Her blouse is pink and cut by a tailor. And her skirt is black, and above her knees, for it was the sight of her legs that had pulled these thoughts from me. I stand, holding on to the same metal pole she leaned on. I wish I could have got off when she did, and follow her up the steps and walk at a distance that did not threaten her, and match her step for step, into the street, along the sidewalk, through the heavy glass door of the building she will enter, and into the elevator with her, and into her office, into her life. But I think of the fear that resides on women's faces when the man who walks close to them carries an identity they cannot penetrate. It is the fear that is painted on their face along with their mascara, even at this early hour, that hinders my daring.

NOT SO OLD,
BUT OH SO PROFESSIONAL

There she would be, sitting, chatting, drinking coffee, as she compared the night's progress and profits, dabbing her lips to remove perspiration, and she would touch the make-up on her cheeks, pale from the time she has spent outside in the night air; and with a glance at the people entering the all-night restaurant, she'd know who they were and what they could be, to her.

I knew the right time to catch her there, to keep an eye on her in this restaurant at the bottom of Church near Granby, an all-night restaurant that had a single line of chairs and tables. Four people able to sit at each. Five at the counter, which ends where the poker slot machines begin. There are plants everywhere, dying, dead, real and artificial. It's a jungle. There is a washroom with a door near the slot machines with no symbol for man or woman on the door. The customers, and the women who sit and chat and dab their faces, they all know what to do when they push that door inwards. I have never entered that nameless door.

There are usually four women who take their coffee together. One looks about fifteen, the more I come to see and know her. And one, the one who looks the oldest, could be no more than twenty-five. She looks like seventeen. But I want her to be twenty-one.

She is terrifying, tall and strong, the shortness of her dress showing the muscles in her calves and in her thighs. I try to imagine her scent. I have tried to imagine her cleanliness. Not *that*, but whether she is meticulous about teeth and underarms.

I wiped that thought from my mind. For many nights, when the temperature was below freezing, she stood in the same square metre of concrete at the corner of McGill and Church, only moving, it seemed, because a Toronto by-law threatened something about loitering. When the temperature was below zero, I was muffled, scarved, and bent at an angle to protect me from the cold. She strode like a sentry in bum-bum shorts.

I imagined that the leotards or pantihose she wore were the identical tint and colour of her skin. Kept her hot. But I changed that opinion one night when I passed close to her. I passed an inch from her, and was glad to be so close, and I saw how young she was, and that her beautiful skin was unprotected by leotards or pantihose. I could see the vapour of her breathing. The light from the pole beside the house owned by the Anglican Church gave her skin a porcelain white sheen. I could smell the scent she wore on her short black dress. I could hear her breathing. And the vapour that came from her nostrils and her mouth mixed with the vapour caused by my anxiety. I looked over my shoulder twice, to see if the two women in cars driving slowly past, had seen me, had known me. I looked over my shoulder a third time.

She was terrifying. It was her beauty and her youth. I could see a mole on the right side of her mouth. I could see the difference in the natural pale colour of her skin and the skin of her make-up. I could smell the perfume she was wearing, beckoning me, clothing me in a kind of comfort and making me strong like a man sometimes wishes to be, and wishes it to be known; a scent that fitted me into a small hurried hotel room, around the corner at Jarvis and Carlton, fitted me between those thighs I had seen for so many weeks from a distance, slipping me in and slipping me out under the nodding approval of the night manager at the desk.

"Hi, honey," she said. I did not want to hear her voice. Nor hear her mission and purpose. I wanted to invent a voice for her, so I said, "How do you do?" I chose this formal greeting to make her know I was different, and to make her say no more.

She was a woman, walking many miles in that square concrete metre, who had seen and heard all kinds of falseness and had known by touch and by size, every form of deceit and depravity. And she had known these things from standing in her small kingdom three cold metres north of the Anglican Church House, which proclaimed from its sign in the front door, that it was reverent and liberal about the station of this beautiful young woman and all she was suffering.

Before I could pass out of her sway, her greeting changed into a song. *Somewhere over the rainbow* and the quality of her soprano pricked me, as if a small drop of water had trickled onto my neck. It was snowing on this night. I could hear the lure, the secret message like a code in the way she sang. I did not find it difficult to see what bliss, what colour, what bodiless ecstasy I could be in for, lying on my back in a cloudy heaven, borne across the tops of the skyscraping buildings surrounding she and me, far, far above the screams from the coupled men who walked like sailors out of the drunken Stables Bar & Ranch House down at the other end of the street. *Somewhere...over...the rainbow.*

"Would you do a thing like that?"

"Would *you?*"

"*Would* you?"

"Not if it was free!"

"They say that it is a fucking experience!"

"I understand if you go with one o' them, man, you don't want go home and hear no shit from you wife. You feel like your skin been stroked by the leaves of a eucalyptus branch."

"A fella tell me that once for his birthday, some friends at this work rented a hotel room, and when they cut the cake, Jesus Christ! A woman came out. He said it went all right, too. But the thing that had him a bit disappointed was that he wanted to spend the whole night, and he couldn't she being on a per diem."

"There no difference between one o' them and a wife, between a woman who do that for money, and a woman you live with. One is cash on delivery. The other, timeless time-payment. Fish is pork, man. I tell men so. The only difference is whether you believe in cash-and-carry."

"But what about diseases?"

"You never heard of a French-letter?"

"For a man to have a wife who is a total woman to him, she have to be a mixture of whore, talker, savior, healer, something of a masseur and something of a seducer."

"Who told you so?"

"Life! I learn it, in the school of hard-knocks!"

"If that's the definition of wife, you may's well marry a whore!"

"What is a whore?"

"You tell *me!*"

"I don't agree with that name, even."

The night was snowing, thick, on the sidewalk, and passing cars clogged the street and brought me close to this woman, no more than the twenty-one years I had imagined her to be; and she was in the right light of winter, the light that makes images fuzzy and sometimes soft, and she looked younger. She was not wearing leotards. I imagined that she drank brandy to give herself warmth. Sauntering within the square metre of her concrete turf, she brushed by me as I moved away from her. I felt sad. I wanted to make a more lasting contact with her. She *must* be filled with brandy or with conviction to be in this smothering cold. But that did not make sense. Brandy would make her miscalculate. That would not do. She was just a young tough kid who loved the cold.

It was a Monday night, days after, and it was not snowing. I was drinking my fourth coffee. I did not want the Vietcong who owned the joint to chase me out. I lit my fourth cigarette, named after an Egyptian king, professing that it contained Turkish tobacco, and therefore was good for my lungs. She came in in a fury, her face reddened by her rage. She threw her handbag down. Its long strap upset a can of pop at her friend's table, and out of her bag came a package of cigarettes. Extra long. And a pink Bic lighter, and a shiny blue packet, the lettering spelling out a name similar to the cigarettes I was smoking. She pushed it back into her black purse. "What the fuck?" she said, not expecting an answer; and she got none. The other woman looked up at her, smiled, and returned to pushing the straw up and down in her can of pop, as if no one had spoken. "What the fuck?"

She got up as quickly as she had sat down, went to the Vietcong, said something to him which I could not hear, walked past me, and went to the stool in front of the slot machines. They were not real poker slot machines, like Las Vegas, which spat quarters out when you made a hit, three Kings and a pair of Aces. These just showed what you could have won. A man wearing a jogging suit, about five-ten, came out from the washroom, a black leather money pouch slung below his waistline making his belly bulge. He covered the room like a security camera. Nothing, no one, escaped his eye. Then, he sat down beside her. He sat down beside her as if he was her cousin, known to her, and needing no introduction. He did not greet her. He just sat, folding his right hand over the three rings he wore on his left hand. And she continued punching the keys on the slot machine. I couldn't see whether she had discarded a King and a Queen and had kept three nines. I would have told her to throw in the three nines and keep the King and the Queen, though they were in different suits. I took my cigarette from the ashtray and I put my white coffee mug down. It had an old smear of lipstick on it. In the mirror behind her, I was able to see her hands, and the man's fist, and the bag, and the three nines which she had kept. If I got the chance to be close to her, I would give her lessons in draw poker.

The man on the stool beside her, now folding his left hand over the three rings on his right hand, to my relief, looked through me, as if I were not there. I didn't want him to think I was there. All the time, in their quiet conversation, conducted by glances and gestures, I was trying to follow any transaction. And in all this time, all they had done was look at each other, careful and diligent to give the impression to the less observant, that he was just a man sitting beside a woman who was punching slot machine playing cards and he, swirling his rings round his fingers, only a man biding his time. And that was all he did, until he got up and moved away from her, in his detached manner. She went on punching cards on the machine. He passed beside me, and without pause, said to my astonishment, as if he were saying a password, "How's the writing racket?"

I waited to see what she would do. And she did nothing. Not to the keyboard. She took a portable telephone from her bag, unflapped the mouthpiece, pulled the thin black wire out, brushed strands of reddish hair out of her eyes, and held that side of her head to the phone. I tried to read her lips, without success: I invented what she was saying, that the man who'd been sitting beside her was pestering her. That did not seem like a reasonable conversation, under the circumstances, so I made her say, "Can you tell me which is higher? Ace, King, Queen, Jack, ten in the same suit?

Or five Queens?" And that was not only unrealistic, but made her out to be stupid, and I did not want to imagine her stupid. I was mulling over these thoughts when I heard a voice behind me. It was the woman whose can of pop had tipped over earlier. She too was talking on a portable telephone.

"Why not find out for yourself?" I turned my head, and just as quickly she looked away, pretending to be studying the potted plants in the restaurant. She was sitting near two large green plastic pots of philodendron and yucca. I could not tell if these plants were made of plastic too. I pretended I was interested in indoor plants. Beside me were a benjimena ficus and a spider plant. A taxicab had just stopped outside the large picture window of the restaurant. I saw the plants move in the windshield, as the driver im-proved on his parking. And in the mirror there was a peace lily and a poinsettia, immediately behind me. I had never noticed these plants in all the weeks of sitting there, watching these women come and go. But now that I was aware of them, they gave the place a softer feeling, almost a romantic feeling, in spite of the cold light from the fluorescent cylinders. And they made the women more appealing; and made the restaurant like a sitting room in an apartment. The fragrance of freshly cut flowers, gladioli with colours raging like flames and yellow roses and pink carnations, and the smell of the restaurant's hastily brewed coffee had the pungency of espresso. The chairs became soft and the arborite and the swivel and the metal became stuffed soft cushions and the chairs had backs against which I could lean and observe what was happening to me. She got up from the slot machine, snapped the wire aerial back into place, put the telephone back into her bag.

She was wearing white tonight. I have no defense against that colour. Nurses and girls going to their first communion, nuns in the hot West Indies, and brides who have not tried out the closeness of sex before their nuptials, doctors who are women, and who dress in white, have always extracted from me an obedience to their demands and orders, to their prayers and missives, to their needles jammed unrelentingly into my arms, whirring machines against my teeth, as I sit obediently in their chairs. For better *and* for worse: white dominates me.

And now this woman, standing before me, amongst the growing plants and those that could grow no more because they were delivered full-grown, and in plastic; she, in a pair of shorts made to look like panties, edged in lace, and fitting like an extra skin that rode on her hips with each step she took in careful measured enticement. On her wrist, a large black strap containing a watch that deep-sea divers, explorers, and navigators of airplanes use. I could not tell the time. The numerals were in Roman. A soft gold heart, in the cruel and sharp fluorescent light, swung at her throat. It was attached to thread-like links of gold. Her breasts were half-covered in white lace, worked into the top of her outfit, and that too was made of white, soft cotton. It was oppressive, irredeemably seductive.

When I recovered from the strong presence of her perfume and her body, and moved my eyes through the urging of her gait, her movement, her stride, her saunter, her walk closer to my table, I saw her legs. They were made more appealing by the long-legged white boots of patent leather, soft as the condom that had slipped out of her purse. Now, she is before me. Now, she is almost touching, close. Now, she is the scent of Evening in Paris, which is just a way of saying that she is overpowering me.

"I'm sitting beside you," she said, placing both hands on her hips the way a woman does when she wants to sit, when she is wearing a dress made from a sheath of silk. "I'm going to sit down with you. Do you mind?"

"What's the difference between one woman who make you pay for sex, cash on the line, and a woman who don't, but makes you pay?"

"The difference?"

"Name *one.*"

"Well, for one thing...."

"Name *one.*"

"I'm trying to think."

"While you're thinking, let me tell you what the differences are."

This was many years ago, in the West Indies; and I cannot even remember with whom I was speaking. However....

I was so nervous and self-conscious that when we crossed the parking lot, cluttered with taxis and their drivers, who spoke no English, I was so aware of their looks of acclaim and conquest that I could not decide whether we should walk on the north side of the short street to my home, or on the side where the senior civil service woman lived. Outside Mr. Tasty Homeburgers, which I had never tasted, I paused to make up my mind. On the north side, lived a lawyer. Beside him, a doctor, an actor, an invalid, a psychiatrist, a businessman of Columbian business, a millionaire who got jobs for temporary bums and short-term unemployed, a jet pilot of the Canadian Armed Forces flying between here and Bosnia, and then my house. If I should walk with her on the south side, I would pass all those cluttered but spying houses that reached up into the sky, higher than the maple trees that grew tall and silent below their prying windows. The house with the senior civil servant woman, then two that housed men and women half-way between society and prison and the mental institution on College Street; past four with tall windows through which they could peer at the parade of men buying women; past one from which no living person ever emerged, but where the newspaper boy pelted the door with his afternoon rolled paper, and then the parking lot that belonged to Ryerson Polytechnical Institute. This lot was always empty, always unsafe under the blazing gaze of a spotlight that chased men who chased women; and some who could not afford a room in the nearby Journey's End hotel. We walked in the middle of the road.

She placed her hand in mine. I could feel the warmth, and the stickiness; and I had to decide whose anxiety was more telling. She walked with a jaunty bounciness which made me unhappy. It said to me that she was glad I was with her; that she had caught me; not in those terms, but the excitement in her walk made me feel there was a conquering satisfaction in her jauntiness. I started to wonder if this was the impression she gave off each time one of those cars I'd seen cruising the street stopped and they conducted the fast, almost wordless transaction. I was still nervous. And I had not even fantasized what I was going to do, and have done to me. This dramatically beautiful woman, whose perfume had struck me in the face, I could not make up my mind about her.

My hand trembled at the wrought iron gate, so I tried with my left hand. It was no better. She shunted me, aside, gently, and on her toes (she was taller than me), and without noise, she opened the gate.

"Gimme the key," she said. I felt she felt we were old friends. I liked her self-assurances. "You're too nervous," she added. I hated her self-confidence. But I gave her the key, and was about to tell her to wait, because there was an alarm, when she said, with the same casualness, "Take off the alarm first. I don't want the cops coming!"

Back in the West Indies, we sat under street lights at night, or under sandbox trees during the heat of the day and the heat of our imaginations, and talked about women. They were always older women. And an older women was any women more than five years our senior. I remembered our conclusions and realized the danger I had got myself into.

"Was it last Friday, or Saturday?" She wondered aloud. "It was Saturday, because I had my first coffee break in the restaurant around ten, and then I had to come right here, across the street, to go to my car, 'cause this bastard was giving me, was trying to give me a hard time, the son-of-a-bitch! So I had to get my *piece*. I was parked right there. In front of your house, and I could see you from the road. You should close your curtains. People can see you from the street. Or turn the lights off." She gave a short chuckle. In her laughter, I was thrown back over the past few days, and there I was returning home with five bottles of red wine and champagne; lugging the large plastic bag of laundry from the cleaners, opening the door about five times to welcome guests, guiding them later into the same parking lot she was talking about; and eventually, at three in the morning, mounting the stairs alone, peeping through the curtains to see if there was anyone standing in the shadow thrown by the young maple tree. I could not remember if the light was left on, last Saturday night.

"And I was scared as hell, in case you were a cop, and I was carrying my piece. But I checked you out through my old boy friend. He's a fucking cop. So, I knew you were clean."

We were inside the hallway, and I was still nervous, more nervous: her intelligence connections, her ability to order things which were confused, scattered, unnerved me. "Tell me something," she said, wedging one heel under the other heel of the white boot, slipping it off, and tossing it under the winter coats on the pegs, below the shelf with the scarves and the gloves. "Tell me something. Would you tell me the truth if I asked you? What are you really doing in the restaurant night after night, sitting, pretending you're not checking us out? We see these things. We got to. You're like those men we see watching us all the time, and can't make up their goddamn minds about what they want." She slipped the other boot off. With a fling of her foot, it landed beside the first one. She pointed at two imitation leather ladies' Wellingtons that had been left behind several months ago by a friend. That's what I told her, "Just forgotten by a friend," and she made herself comfortable.

I went back to those days under the sandbox tree, when we'd declared our intimate knowledge of these things in fantasy and in invention. "You can't indulge in foreplay," Mickey said, who had an older brother who was a seaman, and who had read books from the adults section in the Public Library. He knew everything about the anatomy of a woman, mentioning the names of private parts, the names of menstrual periods and the causes of those periods, and making us uneasy and queasy with his technical language. She stood up. I was nervous and could hardly talk. When she brushed by me in the hallway, walking in her bare feet, she was taller than I was. Then she sat in a chair, her legs relaxed, spread-eagled before me, and I could see lace and the thick belt, like the belts weight-lifters use, and when I looked up, my eyes met more lace. White. And there she was, this young woman, in my house, dressed in white, with the youthfulness of her body before me, for me to do what I liked.

"Am I sitting in your favourite chair?"

"I don't have any favourite chair."

"But which chair do you sit in?"

"I sit in them all."

"You must sit in one more oftener, then."

"This one," I said, standing beside a red chair.

"Well, why didn't you say so?"

I was going to say that since I was the only person who lived in the house, I had no favourite chair. But I was too nervous.

"So, what you want? What's it gonna be?" She glanced at her explorer's watch. "What'd you want?"

"Could we just sit and talk?"

"*Talk?*"

"Would you like some coffee?"

"You have Chinese tea?"

She got up and went into the kitchen, and soon I could hear the sound of things indicating her efficiency. I was beginning to like her.

Mickey had warned me of this years ago. "The most worst thing in the *whirl*," Mickey had said, eating with flourish a slice of coconut sweet bread, "the most serious thing in the *whirl* that man can do, is to tell a woman who picks fares, he want to talk and not to foop!" It sounded so simple that I understood now that I had perhaps brought her into my house under false pretenses.

"Mugs, or teacups?" She sounded the way I imagined a wife would sound, her voice softer than it had been while we walked the dark street, making the house itself softer, and the atmosphere in the sitting room, the dim lights, dim from their forty watt bulbs, just like a room I had seen in a movie, a salon, except that room had thick curtains made of velvet, fleshy and soft as a leaf from the spinach vine in our kitchen garden. The curtains in my house are transparent.

We'll use cups. I love bone china. Got any lemon? Oh, here it is! You sure you don't have some broad living here with you? Or some broad from Molly Maid, cleaning for you? I can smell a woman's presence in this place! You sure?" There was no shrill to her voice, not like the night when she had stormed into the restaurant and said, "What the fuck!"

She sat down, and again placed one leg over the arm of the chair, and I was exposed to all the beauty and the touch and the beating seduction she knew her thighs would bring me. And as she settled in that position, holding the teacup and saucer in one hand, and a cigarette in the other, I found myself sitting forward, leaning towards her, as a student is attentive to a stimulating teacher. Her eyes were constantly moving. From the carpet to the tables to the books that surrounded us, as the plants in the restaurant had provided a surrounding softness to the glare of the fluorescent tubes.

"You read all these books? You like books? I don't read books. I hardly read at all. What I do is watch television."

I was going to tell her that the books were placed in their shelves with precision, and arranged and rearranged by me almost every day, particularly at night, when the house is quiet; and I was going to tell her that it was cheaper to buy pre-cut boards from College Lumber and make the shelves myself than it was to decorate with wallpaper and to choose, but she did not give me time to say these things, she was talking again.

"You know what I really enjoy watching?"

"Movies?"

I just got that in.

"What I really dig doing," she said, "is to watch a movie in French, especially late at night. When I come off my shift. I mean, when I come off the street."

"Did you learn French in school?"

"I didn't take French in high school. And in two semesters of college, I didn't take French, either. I don't speak French. But I like watching movies in French, with the sound off. I find it so exciting. I can sit there and imagine what they are saying. And follow the story. It's nothing. It ain't no big thing to watch a movie when you don't understand the language. All movies have the same plot. A man kills a woman. A woman kills a man. They get into bed. They fuck. They like it. Or they don't. It's like life. That's all it is. No big thing."

"What kind of movies?"

"French. Like I said. Sitting there, in my housecoat, with my feet up, and watching. And a can of beer. Sometimes I turn the sound up, and listen to the words. But I don't understand one damn thing. But I've learned a few words by watching so many movies in French. Late at night, when I get home, I just sit there watching a movie by that fellow with the thick glasses who tells weird jokes. You know who I mean?"

"I know who you mean."

"Him!"

"Yes."

"So, what you want me to do?"

"A drink?"

"Nothing hard, though. My shift's not...."

"Beer? Or wine?"

"Never drink beer, except when I'm watching a movie in French. Wine for me."

"Red, or white?"

"No white unless it's with fish!"

"Bordeaux, or?"

"You got a good Sauvignon...?"

I was watching her legs. She was relaxed. She had taken a comb out of her hair, and her hair fell freely upon her shoulders. She was passing her fingers through it, spreading it out, the action as sensual as I imagined it would be if she were pulling the thin soft silkiness of pantihose over her feet and legs and thighs. My eyes followed the strokes she made through her thick hair, and I felt the passion rise within my body, and it was mixed with anger and frustration, and not a little embarrassment. She was not caressing herself the way I have seen some women pass their hands over their breasts, squeezing the nipples a little to stimulate them and the eyes of the man watching; or how I have seen some women pass their hands over their thighs, slowly, slowly, rubbing faster and then faster still, and slapping them; or even as I have seen some women pass their fingers through their pubic hair to their vaginas, even opening the lips, and doing little stimulating, destroying things to a man's balance. All of these things that women do, I have seen in movies. No. It was not like this. She was just drawing her hands through her hair, a natural function, and that naturalness made it more enticing and betraying and seducing.

"Let me pour the wine." And she was like a woman who had not yet indulged in that ancient practiced custom, that ancient function of preening, the preparatory part of the ritual before the bath. "I can find the glasses. I already saw the wine in the rack."

I was almost beside myself, doubtful of my manhood, convinced I was a prude, someone stunted by birth at birth, someone who had swallowed too many pages of preaching in Sunday school, at matins and at Prayers in high school, someone who had listened, secretly, and out of the hearing of mother and older boys and girls, to the technical talk of Mickey who perhaps had given us too much instruction in this kind of thing, alarmed that I was about to lose my manhood, that raw, undefinable thing that told me, without logic, without instruction, what a man was supposed to do, if he was going to continue calling himself a man. "You ain't no blasted man, man!" A curse levelled at me many times by Mickey. And it was said also, at times of anger, by my mother. Now, in this house, so many miles from that street lamp and from the overhanging leaves of the sandbox tree, I was sitting in a house with a woman whose presence in the house was the consequence of the myth that I was a man. Am a man.

Outside, a car passed, straining the gears. A siren followed. When the siren passed, she sat upright for a moment, I saw her head tilt toward the restaurant where we had been sitting. Then, nothing at all happened. I thought I could hear the wind. We were on the second bottle of wine. I did not know what we were drinking.

Both legs thrown over the arm of the chair, the heavy black leather belt she had worn was buckled around her neck. She had taken her large watch off. And it lay beside her on the end table. The necklace with the heart-shaped drop of gold, remained round her throat.

It was late. I did not know what time it was. I did not think it prudent to look at my watch, or ask her to look at hers. It was comfortable to know that it was late. It was the lateness of the hour that had made me comfortable. And that made her comfortable.

"So, what're we gonna do?" she said, and closed her eyes, although she was alert, and with the glass to her lips.

"What do you want to do?"

"You asking *me*?"

And she gave off a laugh that scared me, it was so sudden and so loud. And then she got up. I thought she was going to leave. It frightened me. She took the leather belt from the chair and put it round her waist. Immediately her hips became large. She raised her arms over her head, straight to the ceiling, and then she bent over, and touched her toes. And then she walked the two paces separating us, and leaned over and touched me on my lips with her lips. Her lips were wet. And sticky from the smear of colour she had applied earlier. And her breath was fresh. And then she passed her fingers, just two of them, across my lips, in secrecy, in fondness, in affection. "More tea?"

And we did that. And drank wine until we started on the brandy.

I had not moved from my chair. Except to go to the bathroom, twice. I was living through a time longer than the hours we'd been sitting, spanning more geography and space than the time we were actually together.

"Did I tell you how I like to watch movies in French, with the sound off, sometimes?"

"You did."

"I guess I did, too. And that I never read nothing, not even the comics? Did I tell you that, too? What time is it? My God!" She picked up her watch, and put it back down. "By the way, I'm Michelle. What's yours?"

"Max."

"Michelle's my professional name. but my real name is Linda. Linda Pearl Mason. It used to be Maisoneuve. French. But my father didn't like the way the Anglos treated him when we lived in Timmins, so he changed it to Mason. Didn't make one damn difference, anyways! Son-of-a-bitch went to his grave hating the Anglos more than he hated fish and chips. You know what I mean? So, you're Max. Max the full name? Or you shortened yours, too?

"Just Max."

"Just Max. Max the Just. Max Justice. Or, Just plain Max?" She took a tortoiseshell case from her bag, opened it, skinned her teeth, closed her eyes and pressed her lips tight, and snapped the case shut. "So, what're we doing, Mr. Just plain Max?"

"Well, I'm sorry, wasting your time. I am really sorry."

"You didn't waste my time. You wasted *your* time. It's all the same to me, if you don't mind me talking business, you know. Well, you know what I mean."

I cowered at the thought of price.

"For Chrissakes, Just Max! You a faggot, or something?"

"I don't think so."

"So, why're you doing this to me? Why me? I could've been in the goddamn restaurant playing the goddamn slot machines! You know what my dream is? My dream is to go to Las Vegas and play the goddamn slot machines for five days and six nights without sleeping! Anyways. What're you gonna do? Should I tell you what you owe me? It's your time, Just Max. It was your call. The ball's in your court."

She got up and sat in my lap. I placed my arms round her soft body, and she leaned over and raised her glass and sniffed the brandy, all the time making her fingers into little feet walking up and down my arm. Each step, though small as an insect's, had the effect of a blow. I could smell her perfume. It was powerful. *Somewhere, Over the Rainbow.*

We remained like this, in the one chair, her walking fingers like a stroking of fresh branches of eucalyptus over my nakedness. I could feel the saltiness of the sea, and the breeze that was, at one moment cool, humid the next; and I could hear birds singing in the trees, and hear the impudent Mickey instructing me, years before the event, in the ways of women who picked fares. And I could feel the water becoming calm, calmer, like at dawn or at dusk, and then there was only surrender, and the abandoning of myself to the stroking of leaves from the eucalyptus branch, and then, as if time had stalled, as if a swell in the sea had risen with the wind, I was driven against the sand, and I opened my eyes.

"Now you owe me, motherfucker!"

JUST A LITTLE PROBLEM

When he came, he was tense. And very courteous. I tried to re-member whether he was always courteous. And when I saw his gal-lantry, which was not contrived, I remembered what a bright boy he used to be, at a time when he was three, and I was twenty-one; when I helped to warm his bottle, and tried to keep the bottle in his mouth and keep him from spitting the nipple out…as he used to spit the milk out; then I would run faster than my mother could, to get the cloth to plug his mouth before the white thick vomit splattered the walls and stained the damask tablecloth; when I used to put him to bed, and the number of times I fell asleep and left him giggling and gaggling, when he was such a darling little boy, the apple of my mother's eye. She got him when she was more than forty-something. She never told us her exact age. "Now, I see him old and thin, and sick, sick, sick," my mother told me on the tele-phone.

He was forty-one. And grown. And tense. And his hands were shaking. And he was very happy to be in Toronto. His hands were trembling. Not only because of the nervousness of meeting me after all these years. "The boy have a little problem," my mother had said, with no sadness in her voice, but with her usual spright-liness; and in the long distance from New Jersey, her voice and her laughter were brought right up to my chair, as I sat drinking a gin and tonic. "Incidentally," she said, "what is that you have there? You drinking?" She could hear the ice cubes, she said, with a tinge of sadness, but she laughed again and said, "The boy can't drink. He can't hold his liquor no more. So I sending him to you to look after. Look after him." And she dropped the telephone. And that was that.

He arrived tense at the place I work. And happy to be in Toronto. "I like it here," he said, five minutes after he arrived. "Man, I'm not going back there!" he said.

So, I introduced him to my secretary, and he bowed to her, and gave her a little pecking kiss, one on each cheek, and she turns colour, and says what a charmer my brother is, and, "I now know where you got it from!" The crow's feet around her eyes disappeared and her countenance was without blemish; and I stood beside my brother, watching this transformation.

We left my place of work and he was saying over and over, what a beautiful place Toronto is, that he ain't going back there; and I wondered if my mother had forgotten to tell me whether he had been in prison, for I could not understand his enthusiasm for Toronto. "I not going back *there*, not me!" he said he needed a drink. I remembered more of my mother's call "Don't let the blasted boy *drink!* Do not let him drink. The blasted boy can't drink no more, you hear me? One sip o' beer pass the blasted boy's mouth, and he like he gone off!" I was laughing when she had said this, and that was when my hand shook, and she heard the ice in the glass. Now, I became tense.

How was I to tell him he couldn't drink? How was I to tell him that I knew he couldn't drink? In our way of doing things, to be able to drink is the sign of manhood. A man who can't hold his liquors, is like a dog. Women despise him. Men call him a boy. And children pelt him with stones.

We walked the short distance to a bar. It was my favourite place in Toronto, dark and friendly, where the Chinese waiter calls me "Mr. Black," and the Jamaican cook greets me, "Man, Blackie, man, wappining?"; and the owner, a man from Ireland, he calls me "Sport." So, I am outstanding in this dark, friendly and colloquial joint. They sell wines and no spirits.

"If he *must* drink," my mother had said, in the same long telephone call from Amurca, "and you could *bet* your bottom dollar that he going-fire one behind your back, or whilst you sleeping. But if he *must* drink, mek him drink beer. *Or* wine."

I decided to order a glass of the most expensive wine, so I can tell him I have no more money, and that way, he will have only one glass. Or a beer.

"Hi Sport!" the owner said. "What'll you have?"

"Meet my brother."

"Christ!" he said. And I knew that my brother was welcome, and that he could run a tab. And this depressed me.

From the kitchen, came the booming voice, "Man, Blackie, man, wappining?" In this atmosphere of friendship I would sit for hours, see the change of staff behind the counter pouring wine, see the change of customers, and when I left, at eleven in the evening or on some nights at one in the morning, the man from Ireland and I would be drinking red wine and chasing it with Jamaica white rum from his private stock. All I could hear was my mother's commanding voice.

"*Don't* let the boy drink!"

"Let's have some Chateau Margaux, man!"

I know Amurcans. They are brave. They are rich. They are bold. The man beside me, my brother, was not behaving like a Barbadian. He had lived too long in Amurca. "Let's try a bottle, to begin with."

"A glass!" I said, to the waitress, thinking of saving him money.

My mother said, in that call from New Jersey, "I don't know when last the boy worked. If you ask me, I think he lost his job!"

We don't sell Chateau Margaux by the glass."

"I have money, man," my brother said. And he pushed his hand into his pocket, and took out a fist of money. I could not count the balled up Yankee dollars: a five, a ten, twenty, fifty, hundred or thousand, they are all the same colour.

The waiter unlocked a door to the cellars, and went down amongst the cobwebs to find the bottle. In the meantime, a thought came into my head. I took up the wine list and searched for this bottle of wine which had sent the waiter into the catacombs of vintage selective prices. My eyes, which have never become accustomed to the darker corners of this bar, roamed amongst the names and I came to *Chateau Margaux* at the bottom of the column *Vintage Wines*. I had left my reading glasses at the office. There was no dollar sign before the price, three digits before a decimal point and two zeros. The price was, as I remember now, *three* hundred dollars and something cents.

I looked at the balled-up Amurcan bank notes in my brother's hand, smoothed them out, counted them three times, asked him if he had more Amurcan smackeroos in his pockets, in his bags, in his attaché case made of crocodile skin, and told him that he had thirty-five dollars Amurcan in his hand. We could purchase two percent of this Chateau Margaux!

"I have bread, man," he said.

Don't mention a word of this. To anyone. Not one word. And I hope he don't hear a word of what I telling you now. I feel foolish even to talk about it, but all I could think about was the telephone calls from Amurca, from my mother, from my four other brothers and a sister; ones from his wife, and dozens from his girl friend. And all were ominous.

"We want you to take him with you, in Toronto. Keep him far from New York City and Brooklyn. Brooklyn going-kill him!"

They told me he had no liver left. He had no spleen. He had too much sugar. He had no control over his body, and little over his drinking. They told me if he got a little scotch he'd bleed to death. "And the boy so bright!" they all said. He was three years into the writing of his PhD in Physical Anthropology, they said. He knew about deads and cadavers and limbs and pieces of a man's head left back from some fatal traffic accident on the Brooklyn Bridge. "Do you know," he told me once, when he was one year into the studying for his PhD, "that there's really no difference between the way a leg o'pork looks and a piece of a man's leg?"

He could use words I had never heard. He could use arguments I could hardly follow. And he was handsome. I became scared. My filial responsibility, my medical responsibility, and the other responsibilities which bound me to him, my brother, were mixed into one feeling of admitted inadequacy. And this was made worse by my acknowledged ignorance of anything medical that had to do with the human body. When I was at school in Barbados, we were not taught anatomy. Science was Greek to me.

And diabetes too, they added. I thought of needles and injections. The voices on the telephone became low and conspiratorial, hushed in whispers, as if people on the line between here and Amurca were listening. "A beer, maybe. Well, even a glass of wine. *One.* But nothing hard, hear? The boy had a sip of beer two days before he left Brooklyn, and bam! He start saying people following him to kill him, people behind every tree between here and where he lives, two doors down from where I talking to you. There are no trees on this avenue."

I thought of my own delight in a martini, in a glass of scotch in a crystal glass. And I like to sit and watch my three decanters, half-full of rum, scotch and brandy; and see how the light of a candle plays on the craftsmanship of the crystal, and wish that I was living in those days when beauty and art and artisanship were common to every man.

And now, with the boy who cannot hold his liquor in the house with me, I had to decide what to do with these decanters, the bottles of wine, the half-full bottles of scotch in the cupboard, and some of the fancy bottles of Cockspur Old Gold Rum and Uisge Baugh Blended Irish Whiskey. I took these fancy bottles from the shelf where he could see them. I put them in the cupboard under the sink with the detergents. I felt a pang of guilt that I was so calculating. "The boy can't handle hard liquor," they had said from Amurca. "If he *have* to, offer him wine, or beer."

Or let him drink himself to death, I was thinking, if he wants to. And then I was sorry I had said it. And into my mind crept all those pictures of men ruined by drink; of men who went to bed drunk holding a shaking cigarette in their hand, and set the place on fire, and burned themselves into charcoal; and some who carried their beloved to this charred fiery grave. And one such photograph stuck in my mind; and it was years ago that I had seen it in a book of drawings by an English painter, depicting the Victorians whom I had been taught at school in Barbados were upright and Bible-thumping models for us in the West Indies, but who hid and drank and hid and fooped, and in this photograph, or woodcut, here was the evidence. A man and his young wife, beautiful as Victorians said Victorians were beautiful, wan and with no blood in her face, with two small daughters hiding in the full skirts of the wife just as the officers of the law were seizing the bed and the centre table and the pieces of silver from the drawers, a family ruined by alcohol. The silver was the gift of his wife's parents, providing hope and health and status to their daughter in holy matrimony.

I was sanctimonious and I was scared. Spleen and liver and diabetes and hardening of the veins, and blood that does not clot. And thinking of liver, I remembered that it was not the similarity of a leg of pork to the amputated leg from a corpse that he had told me about. It was the liver. "The liver we eat," he had said, "is the same as the liver of a man. You can't really tell the difference."

When we were boys back in Barbados, our mother cooked cou-cou, corn meal turned with generous portions of boiled okras and she served this luscious steaming dish with liver, which we call "harslick." There were onions and eschalots grown in our kitchen garden, and tomatoes and thyme and red peppers and butter from Australia. The liver was first fried in a batter of flour, and then steamed in the sauce, with the saucepan's cover on, tight. We ate our bellies full. No, there was no chance that we had mistaken the liver we ate on Saturdays, for the livers he examined in his laboratory clinics. However, I stopped eating liver after that revelation.

I remained concerned with my brother's liver. And yes, his kidneys. They had mentioned kidneys in those telephone conversations from Brooklyn and New Jersey. Spleen and liver and diabetes and veins and kidneys, and blood that did not clot, because of the alcohol.

Don't mention a word of this. To anyone. But I would send him to the corner store where the unsmiling Vietnamese owner puzzled over Chinese cross-word puzzles, and I would ask him to buy the most obscure items I could imagine in order to get him out of the house while I investigated to see what he was sneaking under my nose. And I felt like a thief doing it, like a stranger in my own house. And I could imagine him investigating me investigating him, and discovering I was treating *him* like a thief. It was then that I realized that he had drunk the rum and the scotch from the fancy manufacturers' bottles hidden under the sink. And unlike me, in a former time, he had not covered his tracks by replacing the rum and scotch with water. That was years ago. When I was a student, and was babysitting for my landlord and his wife. The landlord was a psychologist. And the wife taught languages at the University. She died, suddenly, with a reddened face and a burnt-out liver. And we were at my wedding, when the guilt which had not abated with the passing of all these years, gripped me, and in my state of drinking, the worse for wear, and with a loosened tongue, I told him, the only surviving witness to my predatory nature, "Do you remember when I used to baby sit, and you and your wife left with the food on the table, and I would put the things away, and wash the dishes and the crystal glasses, and everything would be spick and span when the two of you returned from the theatre or the ballet?"

"They're indelible in my memory."

He had a way with words that put me ill at ease always. And the fact that he was a psychologist, made me feel he could read my mind and my actions.

"I want to apologize to you. I used to take a slice from your roast, and…."

"And drink my scotch."

"How did you know?"

"And put water back into the decanters. I could have killed you for that. It was only my wife, who…."

And he left it at that, saying, "For better, or for worse."

And all the time he was here, I was dying for a drink. I love to have a bottle of gin in the freezer, chilled and getting thick like syrup, and then make myself a martini, with four of the biggest olives, like small avocado pears, and give the glass a smell of the vermouth. And I like to have a bottle of wine to pour one thick red glass full, strong as blood, to have with dinner; and I like to be able to ramble through the house at night, with the lights dimmed and find the bottle, whether of gin or red wine, or champagne, and pour a drink.

And I need to know there is liquor in the house, at all times, just as our mother needed to know there was always Wincarnis Wine "for building up strength," and castor oil, "for keeping the bowels clean."

I did think of these things, as I walked through my brother's room, trying to pick up the scent of his secret drinking, as I was told by one friend, secrecy is the habit of "people like him." They drink and hide, she said. And you can't hide nothing from them. "They'll find it, and drink every drop. They can't help themselves."

I began to worry. I began to see my brother dying on my hands. Either from the liver which they said from Brooklyn was shot anyhow. Or from the spleen. I have never seen a spleen. And I really don't know which part of the body to find it in. But the word has a collapsing sound in its meaning, whatever its meaning is.

I began to lose sleep. And would stay awake all night, waiting to hear the collapse of his kidneys, if kidneys collapse, and for his cry for help, to take him to the emergency. And I would use a searchlight, no larger than a fountain pen, and walk through the house, after he had said he was going to bed, spotting its pencil point of light, on the floor in the kitchen, round the table, in the hallway, and in and out of the small spaces left by the furniture, cluttering the sitting room. And then I would climb the stairs, soft as if I were a cat, trying to walk on ashes, in silence, in secrecy, like spy, and run the weak shaking light over the pieces of fluff, over the dropped inch of a matchstick, over a careless spot of ash from my own cigarette and from his occasional puff and along the hallway on the second floor, and outside his closed bedroom door. Inch by inch, I moved the pencil light looking for the first clue. And when I realized that I did not know what the first evidence would be, and would look like, I stood outside his door, listening for the slightest murmur to tell me he was drinking in bed, which, according to my friend, was worse than smoking in bed. I sniffed to see if, in fact, he was smoking in bed. All that came from the room was the heavy unmelodious sound of his breathing. But he was smarter than me: and he could have been pretending to put me off the scent.

I pushed the door slightly. And it was blocked. He had placed a valise behind the door. Did he fear me? Did he feel I was going to enter his bedroom, in the middle of the night, and smell his breath? Was this the way he slept, in his own home in Brooklyn? And was it for fear of thieves and men with guns, about which he talked? I decided it was strange. But I would have to think about this at some other safer time.

I continued along the hall, and into my own bedroom. And I shone the light over the walls, all up to the ceiling, in corners, in the cupboards of clothes, in bookshelves, in the pockets of suits and in the soles of shoes. I even shone it in the plastic of laundered folded shirts, in socks and between the two piles of handkerchiefs ironed and folded in quarters. What was I looking for? I was looking for the evidence. They had telephoned from Brooklyn and New Jersey and had talked in whispers, reminding me "not to let the boy drink anything hard, you hear? No more harder than a beer, or *one* glass of white wine, then!"

But one morning as I was leaving for work, he said he was expecting something from Amurca, by Federal Express; and he asked if he would be able to cash "the thing," and what was the exchange; and I told him that I could do it for him and I gave him the cash; and he said, "no problem" and I went to work and forgot about it.

He had no money. He had no job. And I knew, by miserliness, how much change was left from the purchase of milk; what was the change from a container of vanilla ice cream. But I did not tell him that the empty beer bottles in the cupboard could be exchanged for hard, unearned cash. I had put him under "very heavy heavy manners," as my mother said to do.

Once, when I returned from work, he asked me if I needed anything from the Vietnamese at the corner, and I told him no; and he said he needed some butter and some bread and some orange juice; and I said, "See if there's any change." And he said, "No problem." And he returned, wearing his dark glasses, which he had first arrived in, and which he wore during the night, taking them off only about three in the morning, when he came back from his night walk to the all-night restaurant where they sold espresso.

I had forgotten about the dark glasses. And the all-night restaurant slipped my memory. The all-night restaurant has a liquor license.

But this afternoon, he returned with butter and bread and orange juice and a package of cigarettes. The "thing" had arrived by Federal Express. He did not tell me this. And the receipt from the Vietnamese round the corner showed that he had had his own money in his pocket.

Let me tell you, when he was out the pencil searchlight was moving over each item in the house; over the picture frames, in the washrooms, in the toilet bowls and under chairs; checking bottles of mouthwash; checking bottles of cough medicine; checking things and containers that made me see myself, mean and foolish.

And I started to hate my mother; and my sister; and my other brothers and his wife and his girl friend, who had telephoned me, in whispered confidence, and had burdened me with this sick brother, "And if you don't send for him and get him outta Brooklyn, by next week he be *dead* and I know you won't want to have that on your conscience." There was a pause; and then my mother said, "You don't want to say, years from now, *if*. If I had helped my brother...."

The "if" bothered me. If I did not call him and force him to come, he would die. If I did not invite him, the liver would give out. "He hardly got any left back," they had said. If I did not remind

94

him that he is my favourite brother, that it didn't matter he was still working on his PhD in "pure" anthropology, after all these years. If I did not open my arms to him, the spleen would splinter, collapse, and perhaps his blood sugar would roar, or rise, or do whatever blood sugar does. And now that he was here, if I couldn't snatch the liquor bottle from his mouth, the reverse of what I used to do to him when he was an infant, forcing the bottle with a different colour, into his clenched teeth, if I didn't do all these things, I would live with that guilt all my life.

This thing about bottles is very ironical: at the beginning of his life I helped to force a bottle into his mouth, and at the end, which I was sure was at hand, I was entreated to snatch it from his lips.

That night, with the pen-sized torchlight, I searched until the batteries gave out; and I was left standing in the dark. He was still snoring. The valise was behind the door. He had placed it there to protect himself from some devil. They had told me that men who drank in the quantities he did, were visited by devils. Demons, actually, was the word they used. The demons or the devils which stalked his life and his sleep, were now accompanying me as I walked with cold feet on the hot carpets in the house, furtive in my own house, wearied by the spying, and made thirsty by the endeavour.

And then, I remembered. It was the day before he arrived, and I had gone to the liquor store, and had stocked up my cupboard in the kitchen with brandy, scotch, Bombay Gin and wine. But when the urgency in the whispering telephone calls had sunk in, and I was gripped with the unknown terror of having a dying man on my hands, I had no choice but to hide these four bottles. I hid them so cleverly that I forgot their hiding places. I know I did not hide them in the same corner. My mother and his mother, now as I think of this, was the expert at hiding things in our house. She hid things from us, and ended up hiding them from herself. And she couldn't ask our assistance. She hid things so completely, so successfully, new shoes, new belts, candy, her purse when it contained change and gifts at Christmas, from our prying eyes, that she forgot where they were buried in the large dark drawers of the large dark mahogany bureaus in the large, dark house. Once, at Easter, she had to travel back to town to buy presents for the two of us all over again, and she swore and cursed because her corns were killing her. But her dignity and her memory, which we all knew she was losing, could not brook that blow of forgetfulness.

I could not ask him to help me search for the four bottles. I could not bear his telling me that I was getting dotish like our mother. So, in the darkened house, now that the searchlight had given up its life, and as I ran my hands under chairs, under cushions, in dark drawers and feeling the same sensation as when I plunged my hand in the sea, searching for sea-eggs, or for sea-crabs, and knew the damage a spike or a claw could cause, I cursed the day when I'd answered the telephone, and heard the pleading voices of my mother, my sister and my brothers from Brooklyn and New Jersey telling me "the boy need help," and I cursed myself some more for offering that help. And now, I found myself hiding booze from myself in my own house, while I raged in *that* need, with *that* thirst which they had told me he had no control over. That need and that thirst had me now ripping the house apart to find a bottle.

The snoring had stopped. And it alarmed me. And the sound of his breathing became clear, as if the darkness in the house was making it easier to hear. I tiptoed back to the door behind which he lay, protected by his valise, and listened. The breathing was my own. It was quiet behind the door. From outside the room, at the back near the garden, came the laughter of the neighbours. That too was clear and ironical, because it was a reminder of life. But no life could I hear coming from the closed door.

When the laughter beyond the fence died, and the small branches of the maple trees licked one another and touched the fence itself, and the house was still again, and I was thinking of him dead on his back, and the vomit had erupted from his eaten-out guts, bursting his spleen and collapsing his kidneys, wanting to get out, and could not, because it could find no opening and had gone back down into his throat; and when the picture showed my brother with the thick white line from the left corner of his mouth, making his beard a little more grey and making him look older than his short life said he was, in this silent darkness with these thoughts of sudden silent death, came the picture of the hiding places of the four bottles. It was like the relief of solving a crossword puzzle. Or like seeing the solution of a problem in a dream.

They were still wrapped in the brown paper of the liquor store, with the tops of the paper twisted. And I could remember how they felt in my hand, trembling a bit, as I carried them from the brightly lit store. One was in the bottom drawer of the dresser under a pile of sweaters. One was in the cupboard under the sink in the bathroom, in a box that had contained FA Bubble Bath. One was in the basement in an empty box that had contained ABC soap powder. And the fourth was under the mattress of my bed.

I turned the hallway lights on. If the light should wake him, we would talk. I would ask him how I can help. I would ask him if he was ready to go to the doctor to get his blood looked at; and whether he wanted the doctor to check on his sugar. To protect him from this sugar, I had not bought sugar for tea in all the time he was with me. I felt good about that precaution. Not knowing better.

My footsteps, with my new mortal assurances, were heavy enough to wake him. And I wanted to wake him. I went downstairs and turned all the lights on. I was determined not to make my house into a vault, or a hospital ward, not caring to walk around on tiptoe, as if I was beside someone passing from unconsciousness into death. I was no longer mindful of his presence. Patterning my life and behaviour after the precautions to his drinking, I needed a drink, and I was going to have one. And if he awoke, if he escaped from whatever demons and spirits were holding him down, then to hell with them. And to hell with him. I needed a martini. A strong one. A dry one. One with four olives. In my best crystal. And I would have a cigar. The excitement of relief, the end of restrictions. It was like the celebration of something that was new, something that was born. The box of Jamaican cigars was in the top drawer of the buffet in the kitchen.

Bounding down the stairs, making more noise than when the woman who said she loved me came one night unawares, and broke every piece of china and crystal in the house, and would have broken my arse too, had I not learned about discretion and speed and escape, I wetted my lips in anticipation of one Mario Palomino, exquisite Jamaican cigar. The smell of the wood in which they were packaged rose to my nostrils and I was wafted away on the pleasure I would have in pouring myself a drink, the first in the five weeks I had been my brother's keeper. I could taste the martinis with olives large as miniature avocado pears. I could taste the smear of lemon which a senior civil servant in the Federal Government had told me to rub in the bottom of the glass (civil servants know about power and about drink!); and I was going to open the bottle of vermouth secco created by Martini & Rossi, bless their souls, and pass it without pouring, over the two-pint glass tumbler, in which would be chipped ice, and *half* the bottle of Bombay Gin, put down and saved like money for a Christmas present, and I would sit in the wing-backed chair, and listen to Miles Davis, and sip and sip and close my eyes, and savor the taste and see the faces of Italians and Indians and Portuguese and those of whichever race of people grew lemons.

I found the hiding place of the gin. And I laughed at my skill and skulduggery, and how bright I was, how I had hoodwinked him. And I took the brown paper bag from the empty ABC soap powder box, ignoring the smear of powder on my fingers, passing the finger into my mouth, as a woman making cookies passes the spoon with the remains of the mix across her mouth. And it must have been the power of my imagination about the drink, or the size of the ABC soap powder box, which failed to warn me of the disaster. I took the paper bag out of the ABC box. *Do not drink and drive,* the bag said. I ripped the message up. And I stood looking at the empty bottle. The headdress and the crown, and the shroud on Queen Victoria's head, her pudgy face like the countenance of someone who drinks gin, and the bragging declaration that what had been in this bottle was made from a recipe in the year 1761...was she alive then?...was to me, empty and hypocritical and imperialistic like all hypocrisy and emptiness. I had thought that the gin was like its name, manufactured and distilled in India. I imagined Indians, thousands of them coming towards me, with pangas and knives in their hands, screaming and foaming at the mouth in anger and hatred. And knowing I was out-numbered I retreated back upstairs to the other hiding places.

I was as disoriented in my retreat as I had been in my assault. And in retreating there was no solace, no possibility of discretion, and I was never a man who could be accused of valor. The bottle of brandy was empty, too. The bottle of *Père Anselme Chateauneuf-du-Pape* was empty. And like the gin, was placed back in its paper bag, with the top twisted for easy carrying. The scotch was the last I found. I stood looking at the bottle, imagining the times in my long life when a sip of this scotch had been like victory and salvation.

And I went back up the stairs. I did not rush. For I had done that too many times, showing the enemy my intention and disposition. I did not shout, as I had done in times past, foolish with the anger I could hear. I walked calmly and when I reached the top of the stairs I was not even breathing heavy from the exertion. I did not burst into his room. I rested my hand on the doorknob, and turned it, and eased the weight of the empty valise he had brought his things in from Amurca, inch by inch, and felt the door reacting to my push. He was no longer snoring. And I could not hear his breathing, although I could hear from outside, beyond the fence in the garden, the branches of the maple tree brushing against the fence.

And I filled my lungs with the curse and the violence and the chastisement. I blew myself out, in anger like a frog proclaiming dignity and territory and rights. I could hear before they were spoken, the words of abuse.

But all I did was call him by his name. Softly. Almost too soft for the voice to wake him up. The branches of the maple tree below rubbed against the fence. I called him a second time by his name. There was no snoring in the room. The sound of the branches was stifling the sound of his breathing, in case he was breathing. And I felt in the close darkness, to my left, for the switch. And before I turned it on, I called him by his name, for the third time, just as softly, and perhaps, in a different time, lovingly, for I had always loved him. And years ago, when I was twice his age, and he was months only in this world, I used to hush him to sleep and rock him in his bed, and I used to keep the small rubber nipple in his mouth, to get him to drink his milk and mother's love.

The light rested softly on his face, in a kind of smile and covered his entire body in a sheet of contentment. His lips were relaxed, for the smile had painted them too. He was sleeping. And in the light now brighter, in the passing seconds I stood looking down on his body, fully dressed, as I had seen him hours earlier, I saw the thick line of white foam that had started inside his mouth, and was now dried to his face.

THEY'RE NOT COMING BACK

On the second night, the day after it happened, the home was dark. She was surprised to hear the six o'clock news on television as she closed the front door. She could not remember whether she had left the television on for security or whether she'd wanted to hear voices in the empty house when she came home. The bottles in the big brown paper bag nearly slipped from her hand. The liquor store was closed at six. The bottle was her sustenance for the night. She was a Catholic. She went to church irregularly, but devoutly, if that is possible. And always, she read books of devotion at night or *The Lives Of The Saints,* especially when she needed something steadfast in her life. She was doing well: confident in her new job; saving when she could; dressing smartly, and she kept in touch with her friends and family. What grieved her was her husband.

She'd always said it was a bad marriage, but she could offer no certain act, no one thing for blame. She knew she was unhappy. And that was the only important thing. When she'd left him in the house, her house, the house her parents had "given" them for one hundred dollars, she said it was a decision she'd made three years earlier. But she'd taken with her, though she'd tried differently, countless problems from the small renovated bungalow, built in the same style as the one she now rented: she'd taken with her pains and anger from the past two years, unpaid bills and balances on his credit cards, personal debts now changed into consolidating loans;

her fifty percent obligation to all these debts; and the two girls, one sixteen, the other nine.

The new house was now full of their absence. The girls were as beautiful as their mother, though larger in their limbs, and more mature and grown-up than their ages suggested. It showed on their faces and in their actions, just as their mother's pains and anger showed in her face. And the fact that they were not here tonight, welcoming her, as they did every other night, with complaints about the school day and each other, filled her with anxiety. She was a woman waiting for something bad to happen. She did not know what it would be, but she was certain it would happen. And there was the emptiness.

Five days ago he'd said he would come and take them from her, and drive them to their home, now his, with his young daughter, only two months old, and his new woman, their step-mother, who occupied the space she had said was sacred, the space that was the result of the sweat that had poured off her father's face while he worked for twenty years digging trenches, lifting heavy objects until the strain pulled something in his body and made his testicles grow large, the size of a grapefruit. Her father and mother had given her the small bungalow as a wedding present; marrying that "Bastard, Kit, 'cause I can't tell you I like the bastard and the way he treats my daughter;" and, it was where her mother and father had lived, in the basement, for the first years of his retirement, until they moved to a little place in Florida for six months. They lived in a home for the aged the other half year.

Yes, five days ago he said he would come and take them. It was an experiment. It was for the sake of the two girls. The elder child had told her mother she wanted to live with daddy. The previous Sunday, when he'd brought them back earlier than usual because he had "things to do," just as she was preparing a dinner of roast beef and mashed potatoes with thick brown gravy, the old daughter declared, "I want to go live with Dad." She heard the words go into her heart, into her abdomen, into her womb. She went over and over all the things she had done in the sixteen years of her daughter's life, doubting her methods of bringing her up, doubting whether she had put the child to lie on the right side, the correct side, whether she should have persisted and fed her from her breasts in spite of the gland problem that had developed. No one ate more than the first spoonful of supper, and then the roast beef with mashed potatoes with thick brown gravy was shoved aside.

"Can we go to the store and get chips and bubble gum?" the sixteen-year-old said.

She knew what it meant for them to come home from school at three or half-past three five days a week and find the bungalow empty, with the lights turned on for company, and the radio blaring out their favourite rock music. She knew what it meant for two young girls to be in this neighbourhood in this house that stood in a long line in the long street, identical in red brick; and she knew too, what it meant for them to be alone in the house, large and eerie on this side of the street of men who did not go to work during the day, men who worked during the night and were home during the long boring day.

A man of forty-nine had entered a bungalow when the single parent was at work, taking possession of both the house and the child. It was on the front pages and on television. The little girl was fifteen years old. Blood stained the street for months while mothers wrought their hands and the police, diligent as worm pickers, trudged in the snow and found nothing but a brown plastic haircomb. She knew how it felt. She knew how it could happen. She had left her children alone one night to meet a man. During the passionate hour with the man she had bristled with resentment because she did not have the leisure to enjoy making love, which she loved to make, and was filled with guilt and doubt: could the sixteen-year-old look after the nine-year-old, and remember to keep the television loud, and remember not to answer the door, and if she answered the telephone, remember *not* to say, "Mom is not here;" but say, "She's busy at the moment." These fears left her shaking in all her limbs, so long untouched, so long tense, so long pure.

At the age of seventeen, because the boy with whom she was in love for life had left the small town to make his fortune in the city, and had not said he would return and take her with him while he made his fortune, she gave up boys, and gave up all pleasure and buried herself in books, and knelt in the crimson draped confessional and whispered to the priest that she was entering a nunnery.

"I want to enter a nunnery," she said, hardly audible, so great was her devotion.

The priest whispered, "You want to be a nun?"

"I want to enter a nunnery."

She smelled the incense, she heard liturgical music in her heart. She felt the boy's hands on her breasts, her body shaking like she shook the night when she'd left her children alone.

"I want to enter a nunnery."

The priest, knowing young girls, told her to think about it for a week and come back. When she did go back, to the same priest, in the same small box, with the same crimson velvet curtain, she said to him, in the same whispering voice, "Father, I think I am pregnant. But he has promised to get married before the baby shows."

"Are you still thinking of becoming a nun?"

The house was dark. She could hear her own footsteps on the linoleum, and her heels sticking to it because she had not mopped up the orange juice and milk spilled on the last morning at breakfast with her daughters. She dropped her briefcase, rested the brown paper bag on the table, and walked towards her bedroom. Normally, she stopped in the kitchen, put her manicured hands into the thick oily water full of plates and saucers and coffee mugs and knives and spoons and her one crystal martini glass. She washed the three sets of dirty dishes, unable to understand why there were so many, and she would stand looking at them, plates half-buried in the murky water. When done, almost every evening, it would be close to ten o'clock. No one would have an appetite: neither she nor the two children.

Free of that chore, she headed for her bedroom, and felt the emptiness there. Sometimes the younger child, tormented by the older, would seek refuge on her mother's bed. It was a welcome show of affection, even when she had to sort out the quarrels and secret beatings. Tonight, there was no child on the bed. And in a flash of hope and forgetfulness, she wondered why.

She went down the wooden steps, almost too narrow even for her small body, into the basement, and along the cement floor past the furnace-room door to the largest bedroom, the room her elder daughter had commandeered when they had moved into this house. The bed was made. In the middle of the single mattress was a book. The girl was always reading. At seven o'clock on that night, she had just put the book down when the car horn sounded. The book was open and turned down. She had always scolded her daughter about damaging the spines of books that way. She went to the small closet and opened the door, saw the empty shelves, and the wire hangers, some of them bent into shapes to suit her small-size blouses, brassieres and denim jeans. On the bookcase, there was only a white envelope. Nothing was written on it. A ballpoint pen sat beside the envelope.

All around the room, cool in the summer and warm in the winter, large and bright for a basement room, her eyes wandered, picking up her daughter's presence, her movement and posture, the sound of her small feet when she walked in her bare feet after her bath, when the floor was spotted by water. She sat on the bed, and before she rose, she turned her face away from the bed, left her right hand on it as if she were patting it good-bye, as if the closeness of the body that slept in it was still on the blue sheet patterned with daisies.

She hurried back upstairs. At the top of the stairs, she paused, as if catching her breath, but she was young and in good health. She paused and put her hand to her head, to think of the heavy presence in the empty house, and of loss.

"Are you sure you want to do this?"

"Sure!"

"You realize of course that it could be seen, perceived that you are giving your children up, and…."

"I'm not *giving* my children up."

"I know that. But."

"Suppose, just suppose the arrangement is for a few months, till I catch myself, till I am more in control of myself. And we can have an agreement saying that it is for a few months and at the end of this time, they'll come back to me, and…."

"I understand what you mean, and I understand what you want, but I have to advise you that the perception…."

"The perception is one thing. I know about perception. But the reality is that he's taking them for a trial period. It is the decision of my daughter to go and live with her father."

"What're you going to do with the little one? Send her, too?"

"How can I separate the two of them? What is he making me do? What is he up to? Does he want me to send the older one to him, and me keep the younger? I won't have it. I won't do it. I don't trust his motives. What does he want me to do?"

"Suppose…suppose before the time ends, they want to come back to you? Suppose, only one wants to come back before the trial period ends? Or, now that you're moving to a more economical place, suppose before the five-month arrangement ends, one of them wants to live with you?"

"You mean...?

"Yes."

"You mean *that*?"

"Or when the time ends, they don't want to stop living with their father?"

"You mean, they're *not*?"

She took a Kleenex from her purse and spread it on her knee, and then put it to her face. She had been biting her lip. She could feel her muscles tighten.

"How's your concentration at work?"

"Fine."

"And your nights?"

"Just fine."

"You know, a little snort...a spot of brandy. Are you sleeping well?"

"My doctor gave me something."

"Sleeping pills?"

"Something to relax."

"To relax you? I'd be careful."

"I'm fine."

There was a slip of yellow paper, a paper a little bigger than a postage stamp, in her shoe. She recognized the handwriting of her sixteen-year-old. She closed her eyes, refused to read it, feared its message, and tore it from the sole of the shoe, balled it up, put it into the pocket of her skirt. She had arranged all her shoes at the bottom of the cupboard according to the fondness she had for them; and she ran her hand along the metal bar that held the wire hangers with her dresses. She wrenched the hangers to the left, not liking how they looked, and then wrenched them in the opposite direction. She looked at her bed, saw how large it was for the room, and promised to call her sister and take back the smaller bed and mattress she had left there. She looked around the bedroom, hating that she was forced to move out of her home, more comfortable than this even when they had been four plus a dog that had fleas; and two cats.

Her eyes were sore; she must change her lens. She blinked, held on to the top of the dresser, placed her right hand, the third finger, to her eyeball, flicked her lid, and extracted the miniature piece of plastic; and she placed her left hand, not seeing clearly, on the white bottle that contained lotion, and her fingers touched a small slip of paper, the same yellow colour as the first, and before she used the lotion, straining her eye to see, she saw the handwriting again, and this time, she had no excuse for not reading it.

"*Mummy, I still like you. Your daughter.*"

She used no Kleenex this time. She allowed the suppressed feelings of hurt and disappointment that had welled up for three days to spill out: and she sat on the edge of her unmade bed, allowed the tears to fall, and did not seek to control them.

Why didn't she write "love?" Did her daughter not love her? Why didn't she say she loved me? She felt the parting note was too formal, too distant, after only three days. On the door of the fridge was another note. It repeated the same longing and liking. And when she took the plastic holder with the ice cubes from the fridge there was another note. It was frozen into the ice.

The martini she made was pure gin. Luckily, she'd found Bombay Gin. And she had an old bottle of olives in the cupboard. If she was in any doubt about the potency of the pills her doctor had prescribed, she would wash them down with the first martini.

"In a way," she said to herself, "in a way it's good the kids are gone. I don't have to worry about supper." She corrected herself. "If they were here, I would not be able to have this martini." She liked the revision.

On the night she'd left the girls unattended, going to see the man, she'd known she was going to have sex, not to make love, because as she said to herself, "I can't make love to a man I don't know." It had been such a long time since she had had sex with a man. It had happened only with her husband, it had happened whenever he came to see how the kids were taking it; and each time she broke down. He promised to change his ways and told her that it was "just for a time," and that he intended to give her some space and distance. In that confused understanding, he took her upstairs into her new bedroom where her clothes were still in boxes and some of them strewn over the uncovered mattress and he took her and did not pay attention to the spots and smudges on the gray-striped single mattress, so thin that he thought he could feel the boards of the bedstead in his steady, hard, unloving pushing against her eager body. Yes, it was to have sex, to remind herself that she had not entered the nunnery and that her body, as the body of a woman, needed that nourishment. He knew it. And she knew it.

She believed that with the other man, whom she has not spoken to nor seen since that hectic night, the sinfulness of the act was mollified by the urgency of her body's need. She was not going into a nunnery. And after all, she said, breaking the speed limit to get back to her unattended children, "I'm a free woman."

When she got back to the house, the sixteen-year-old was sitting on the couch in the living room. The television was a steady scene of falling snow. When she saw the screen, it reminded her of the plunging water at Niagara Falls. In the lap of the sixteen-year-old was the nine-year-old. Both were wrapped in sleep. Each had a smile on her face, oblivious to the risk her mother had taken. Both were in the rapture of sleep, as she had lain in rapture for five minutes in the man's arms, after he had screwed her, and had sunk into a doze.

She went back over these things. The clothes she had worn to work for the past five days were dropped over chairs, and some of her underclothes were draped over the back of the toilet. The shoes she'd worn were scattered, kicked off as soon as she had come home. "Feet killing me!"

She had seen the state of the kitchen, the uneaten meals, the fragments of toast, the dishes left unwashed in the stagnant water. Ashtrays were filled with cigarettes stubbed out, twisted, and some were hardly smoked at all. In some cigarette packages, she had left matches and cigarettes and telephone messages which she never returned.

The liquor she'd bought, the brandy, the Tanqueray Gin, and the sparkling wine, stood arranged in a triangle of bottles in the cleared kitchen counter space. The water glass was filled with cubes. The crystal glass, the only one she had washed out of the cluttered sink, sat sparkling among them.

The first martini struck her stomach, exploding all the hurt and pain and self-crucifixion at the sight of the notes from the sixteen-year-old, notes pinned against her heart. She walked through the house, ignoring the evening news on the television, and the announcer screaming about the success of the Blue Jays who were playing in Oakland. She sipped her martini. She could not feel the touch of her feet on the carpet. "I have to vacuum." Dust had risen, she could see it in the beam of light from the floor lamp. She swore to herself that she would shift a framed photograph, remove a dried bunch of flowers. Everywhere she looked she saw a note left by her child. She had three more martinis and cried herself to sleep.

She fell asleep on the couch. Very early the next morning, the dishes were still unwashed. She found more notes from the sixteen-year-old. One was in her panties in the drawer. She discovered one stuck to the blank cheque in her book that was to be sent to the landlord. She sat down and drank two martinis, and as they did not stimulate her, she poured herself a brandy, looking at the morning news, and a game show and a talk show. She was about to take a sleeping pill but realized it was nine in the morning. For the second time that week, she called in sick, saying she had to take the kids to the doctor. But they had been with their father for three days, now. She took *The Lives of the Saints* from under the jumbo box of Kleenex and opened it, but before she had read the first paragraph, her vision became blurred by the tears. She was thinking of sin and of the time she'd sat in the small confessional and whispered to the priest, "I want to enter a nunnery." She cried and she wondered if she was losing her mind. And how was she to stop it?

She filled the house with noise from the radio, the television, the stereo. But her best balm was the martinis. She loved martinis, and drank them in generous quantities. They were a part of her sophistication. Other women, her sister and friends in the office, drank white wine. She held that for a woman to drink martinis showed a sign of class.

Now, she was sitting in the living room on the large couch. The gin was gone. She passed her hand over the couch's silk material and noticed stains left by her children. She made a mental note to wash them with detergent and a cloth; better still, send the whole damn thing to the cleaners. No, not the cleaners, to the upholsterers. And then she decided that the other couch, which was too large for the living room, should be sent to the upholsterers too. Then, she made up her mind to throw them out and replace them with furniture that she, as a new woman, demanded. A new, fresh, virginal beginning. She looked at the coffee table, and then at the end table, and the large dining table, and the television, her reliable friend, sworn to keep her company. All were discarded. She was sipping Courvoisier. She became tense, with a pain that entered her stomach, and went up into her chest. She thought of stress. She thought of ulcers. She thought of her heart. She inhaled deeply six times, taking deep, deep breaths, trying to hold them. She knew people held their breath in these circumstances. She couldn't. She put the snifter down on the coffee table and said to herself, "These things could be my death." She stood up and felt better. She poured herself a more generous Courvoisier, in which floated four snippets of lemon peel. She had eaten a bottle of green olives.

It was late now. Still, only half of her body was tired. Fatigue did not touch her mind. She thought of things to do the next day at work; she thought of plans for the transformation of her bungalow; she thought of plans, not really plans but plottings, to get her children back with her; and she thought of the new richer life she would lead, as a result of this rebirth.

The movie on television was in black and white. There were women in long dresses that reached to the floor. And men were wearing formal clothes, with stiff collars cutting into their necks, just below their chins. Their necks were red, though she could not see that colour; she had seen such men during her holidays in Florida, when they spoke to her. And there were servants coming and going. She had spoken to women like them at the bus stop. She could picture herself in that grand living room. The amount of drink being served made her comfortable. It was her place. She was born to be like this.

Five months' pregnant with her first daughter, he'd been kind and attentive. He'd sat with her on the hospital room floor where she and six other mothers-to-be were on mats, and one day a week they'd pretended that they were giving birth. He would breathe with her, rub her belly, and have an erection, impatient to take her back home to jump on her belly, sometimes forgetting that his seed was buried already inside it.

And he was in the room when the pains really started. And he held her hand when they increased. And when his first daughter was born, he saw it all, and did not leave the room until he had to. That night he called her mother and her father, her sister and brothers, and distributed expensive cigars. And then he went home.

He was home for fifteen minutes before the woman arrived. She parked her car in their garage. She went through the front door, straight to the bedroom. The pink baby booties, bonnets, sweaters, nightgowns and suits lay undisturbed at the foot of the bed, which his wife had made minutes before he had driven her to the hospital. And the infant's garments remained undisturbed, by some miracle, while he "fucked the living daylights outta her," which is how he put it to his friend at the desk next to his the following morning, holding open the almost empty box of Tueros cigars, celebrating his first-born child.

She heard about this years later from her husband's friend when they were no longer friends, when the friend wanted to assure her that that friendship had ended, after he made a pass at her, as he told her what a bastard her husband was, had been, and would always be. It was the same man she had gone to on that might when she had left the nine-year-old in the baby-sitting hands of her older sister.

She gets up, tired and sore, and she takes up the telephone.

"How are you?" It is her mother she is calling. "I haven't spoken to you in a long time," she says. And she has to repeat her words, because her mother cannot hear them distinctly.

"You been drinking, darling? I know what you're going through. And a glass *does* help. I won't like to know you're overdoing it, though. Are you all right?"

"I'm fine. I'm fine."

"You know, darling, when you were a little girl, and you came home from school and I would ask you how school was, you always said, 'Fine,' just like you're saying now. Everything I asked you about, you always said, 'I'm fine.' I knew things weren't fine. Because things're never fine, all the time."

"I'm fine."

She could not remember if she had asked her mother to come over. She could not remember when it was that she had made the suggestion, if in fact, she had.

She went into the bedroom and took the plastic vial from the medicine cupboard. She did not have to look at the writing on the bottle. And she did not have to spend any time selecting this bottle from all the others there: aspirin, vitamins and pills prescribed months ago for other medical ailments, which she never completed taking according to the doctor's orders.

She took a few, put them into her mouth, and took a sip of her brandy. She passed a brush through her hair. And she examined her face in the small looking-glass in the bathroom. She cleansed her face with Noxema cream, applied make-up and even brushed one of the four colours from the Cover Girl case across her cheeks.

It was past midnight. She'd made her face pretty. She'd made her appearance appealing. And she did this even though it was only her mother coming over to see how she is. And she knew that her mother would be gone in fifteen minutes, for it is so late; and there is really no need to fix herself to meet her mother. She *is* her mother. And mothers understand that love and appreciation are not measure in this kind of preparation.

She raised her skirt, hooked her fingers into the elastic at her waist and lowered her pantihose. She chose a fresh pair. The pills started to make her feel relaxed. She will sleep tonight. The pills and her martinis. And she will usher her mother out, nicely, after a few minutes. Before she put her panties on, she took her silk dressing gown from the nail behind the door of her bedroom. It was rich in colour, a pattern of dragons and beasts that could be from the sea or the vast land of China. It was warm on her soft beautiful body, no longer old and tired, as it was a few minutes ago when she rose from the couch. She drew the skin-coloured silk underwear over her legs, and she felt a slight irritation. A piece of paper. And she pulled them down, and a page from her personalized stationery, folded into the size of a large postage stamp, fell out.

She unfolded it, passed her eyes over the uneven letters, in capitals, the uneven pencil strokes telling her, *"We are not coming back coz you send us away."* when the doorbell rang. She jumped. She wondered who would call at this hour? She wondered if it was her husband. She wondered if it was the man, her husband's friend. She wondered if it was her children. She had forgotten she had spoken with her mother ten minutes ago.

She crept to the door, looking through the hole and saw the disproportioned face of the woman standing on the other side. She looked old, and ugly from the magnification, and frightening. But it was the eyes, her mother's eyes, that told her she was safe. She was safe again, safe always when she was with her mother. She was safe in all the those years of her bad marriage whenever her mother called, or came over, and sat with her, holding her face in her lap and sometimes, her mother would have her lean her head against her shoulder and pass her hand over her forehead, as if she knew she had a headache.

The note was still in her hand when she opened the door, taking the chain, pulling back the bolt, unlocking the deadbolt.

"What have you got there, dear?"

She showed it to her. "My dear! Leah wrote this?"

She did not answer. Her body was weak, too weak from the exertion of words and explanation. And water had already come eyes.

"The *little*...."

Her mother did not complete her sentiment. There was no need to.

"Where're you going this hour?"

She had noticed how properly her daughter was dressed, hair in place, every strand of her dark brown hair; and the make-up and eye-shadow; and she mistook the silk housecoat for a cocktail dress.

"You young people wear such crazy styles, child, I thought you were on your way out! What would make Leah write a thing like this?"

"You want a drink, mom? I only got gin."

"Your father would think I was out to meet a man, at my age!" And she laughed her full-throated laugh. And her daughter laughed too. And was happy for the duration of that laughter.

"Oh, mom!" she said. "Oh, mom!"

And then tears engulfed her, and washed over her, and gave her the feeling of holiness that she had known in her childhood years of accepting the ritual of being a young Christian-minded child. She knew that powerful feeling that swept over her when she attended Mass, like the warm water of the sea when she and her mother went on their holidays. And she could feel the spirit she knew was inside her body when she knelt and said her personal prayers, after the priest had given the Benediction.

"Oh, mom!"

"What're you doing to yourself, eh, child?"

"Oh, mom!" She reached for the snifter.

"Why don't you put an end to this, dear?"

"Oh, mom!" She said in the whisper she'd used when she said she intended to enter. the nunnery. "Have I disappointed you, mom?"

"You are my daughter," she said. And drew her body closer, and rested her head on her shoulder. "You smell good. What is it?"

"I'm using Chanel now, mom."

"That's a good scent."

"Oh, mom!"

"Now, first thing in the morning," her mother began, passing her hand with the three gold rings on the wedding finger over her daughter's forehead, and then along her neck, "first thing in the morning, you and me, we're going to see somebody for you to talk to." And she could smell the scent, and the shampoo her daughter had used. And she could feel the muscle on the left side of her neck. And she could feel the softness of the silk of her house-coat.

The time passed slowly. Her mother sat silently and paid no attention to the movie on television. Soon there was snow on the screen. All she could hear was the taking in and letting out of breath from her daughter's warm body and the sudden, short star-tled moving of the body. Once, instead of a shudder, there was a sigh. She went back over the years of struggle with the six children she'd borne the man she loved, and still loved; how she'd cut and contrived and got them all through high school, and all but one in college and university; attending graduations and birthday parties, and weddings and christenings.

And you were always my favourite, out of all the children I bore, you were always my star, and I can still remember the nights I stayed up with you, seeing you through measles, mumps, cutting your teeth, toothache, earache, everything, until you met that man you married and threw away your life, you the star, my favourite out of all the children I carried in my womb.

And time passed without her notice, for she did not know the body was no longer so warm, and she thought of raising the thermometer, these bungalows where the workmen worked so fast and didn't know one thing about insulation. Time, passing without sound. And there is no longer the spasm that tells of life, and there is no longer the soft whisper of sleep.

It is quiet. And this quiet is felt not in the motionless sleeping body she is holding, not from anything inside this house, but through the sound of the leaves and a branch rubbing against the house. And it becomes cold. Her own body is cold and she draws her daughter closer still to her body.

In all the time, and with all these children, all of them out of my womb, you, you Claudette were always my star, and my joy. Out of all of them, I loved you the most. All these years, all these years.

But this time, it is different. The weight is lighter, but the burden is heavier. Her right shoulder is numb, bearing this sleep that is like a solution. First thing in the morning, I will take you to somebody to talk to you.

It is still. It has been like this for awhile now, and still she continues to pass her hand with her wedding rings on it over and over her daughter's forehead that smells so well of Chanel. And her hand, like her shoulder, loses its life and feel, the circulation gone out of it, until she opens her eyes. And looks. And sees the beautiful tranquil face. "Sleep. Sleep, my darling."

Her face is soft and relaxed. There is a smile across her lips. Her lips, the smear of the lipstick. The mascara. Her face is soft and relaxed; and the beauty that defines it is young and innocent.

"Sleep."

THE CRADLE WILL FALL

We were sitting on the sand. The sand was the same colour as the shell of the conch. The conch was empty, dead and old. And it had been left in the sea, for days, perhaps months. It could have been years. Sometimes when we were at home, a few hundred yards from the beach where our fathers and uncles had sat years before us, an uncle had been dragged up filled with water, drowned and blue, and someone would put this same conch shell to his lips, and blow a signal, a tune, a warning of things to come. We were sitting on the sand and the sun was going behind the water far out, beyond the power of our eyes to focus; and it was still hot, and the water was washing in, lazily and without waves; washing our bodies.

Out bathing pants, as we called them, were made of khaki. They were the pants we'd worn to high school. Now, they were tattered. They were torn in many places in the shape of an L. They were cut down, and they reached almost to the knee. When they were soaked in salt, they became heavy, and stuck to our bodies.

We were sitting on the sand. The water mixed with sand made the sand the same consistency as the Cream of Wheat porridge our mothers made us eat for strength, to make us men.

John had stepped on a cobbler, and the cobbler, John said, was angry at him. It broke off about ten black needles into his foot. The ten needles were visible. Just the tops. I could see them clearly against the dark pink of his sole. All ten were in the heel of his left foot. He had told me that he was "double-jointed." He'd shown me how double-jointed he was. The evening before, while sitting on the sand, he had grabbed his right leg with his right hand, and put it over his head. I had closed my eyes, expecting to hear his joints break. But nothing happened. All I could hear when he did this trick was water lapping against the pink shell of the conch. And then he did the same thing with his left leg. I closed my eyes again. And when I opened them, I thought John had turned into a soldier crab. His joints did not break. I knew then that he was "double-jointed." And I told him that his limbs were made out of rubber.

"Rubber?" he asked me. "Like the rubber of our inner tube?"

The inner tube, patched in many different colours, was just then drifting out to sea. The tide had come in, and a wave falling back over itself had dragged it, like a thief, out of our reach. John was able to swim, but the ten black points in his pink heel were stinging him. He had wanted to teach me to swim, but he had forgotten. And anyway, the sea was always too rough.

"The tube! Man, look the tube!"

And I got up, and ran towards the water. And stopped. And thought of the water coming up to my shoulders, and then my head, and then my mouth. And I saw again, as if it were happening in front of me, my uncle's bloated body, filled with sea water and with some moss in his mouth, heavy and dead, while the other fishermen dragged him the same way they had dragged a shark up the beach, along the sand, leaving the trail of body and legs over the sand the colour of the shell of the conch. That Sunday afternoon, someone blew the conch shell too.

"The blasted tube, man!" John was hopping on one leg, waving his hands and pointing. "Swim, man! Swim out and save the blasted tube!"

I remembered the "moses" my uncle used to push into the sea, and guide into the deeper water to reach his anchored fishing boat;

and I remembered how he would hop into it, and before I could blink my eyes twice, in the twinkling of an eye, as my mother would say, the "moses" would disappear amongst the climbing waves, higher than any hill in Barbados, and then I would hold my breath, and when I released it, the "moses" would be like a hat thrown into the sea, or a leaf, dancing in a frolic upon the steadying waves. Then, he would reach the fishing boat, *Galilee*. He was a deacon in The Church of the Nazarene, when he was not catching jacks and sprats, flying fish and sharks, dolphins and congo-eels. He never ventured into the sea on Sundays except early Sunday morning, to fetch back fish-pots from the rewarding sea, pots filled with after-morning-church dinner of barbaras, cavallies, ningnings, sea-eggs when the season was right – the name of the month ending in "er"; and once, to our religious joy, a lobster. It weighed twenty pounds, one ounce.

"A twenty-pound one-ounce lobster, man?" my aunt had said, hefting the thing in her left hand, with a stick in her right, ready to strike it dead as it wriggled big and little claws close to her face. "Man, whoever hear of a lobster that weigh twenty-pounds, one ounce? You not 'fraid God strike you dead? And on a Sunday morning, to-boot?"

"Well, not that in a real sense I mean that this lobster tipped the scales at twenty pounds, avoirdupois, plus one ounce," he said, relishing his use of big words. He had no scale, and never relied on them; but weighed everything, fish, potatoes and mangoes by hand, by hefting them. "When I say it tipping the scales at twenty pounds, one ounce, assuming I did-have a blasted pair o' scales, it is only a way of speaking, girl. Only a way of speaking!"

It was however just two weeks after that Sunday, that they brought him back, as if he were a shark he himself had caught, out in the darkness, putting an end to his fishing on the Sabbath, as he called Sundays, although he did not know what it meant.

"Swim out! Swim out!"

John's voice rang in my ears, but I was seeing the "moses" drifting in the trough of waves; then the *Galilee*, then the darkness, then the blowing of the conch shell that killed the smaller signals from the doves of the wood, and then the bruised sand over which they dragged his body, bloated by water, bloated more than my teacher had told me was the proportion in a human carcass, and then the darkness.

"Swim out! Swim out!"

I stood my ground. I saw the black tube do the same dance as the "moses." I saw it disappear. I saw it reappear. I saw it get small and smaller, smaller still, until it was the same size, the same black mark as the cobblers in the pink skin of John's heel. That was the last I saw of the tube. That was the last time I remember sitting on the sand with John. That was the last time before I left the island, and John soon behind me, when we did almost everything together; or had it done to us; birth, baptism, christening and confirmation; leaving elementary school for Combermere School for Boys, a second-grade school that trained senior civil servants; joining the choir of St. Michael's Cathedral where we learned to learn Roman numerals before we could follow the announcement of Psalms at matins; scouts, cadets, Harrison College, a first-grade school for boys and for turning us into barristers-at-law; and University. America for me. Somewhere else, for John.

I was walking in the snow. The snow was deep. And my legs were heavy, and I felt I was walking in frozen water. I had not remembered to take my shoes to the shoemaker. And I was slipping. I was moving one heavy foot at a time, at the same pace as an old blackened sail I used to see far out at sea, on that same beach where we sat, fifty years ago, counting the steamers and lady boats which brought strangers to our shore. It was about four o'clock, a time when there is still a sun overhead, but today, in January, at noon it feels as if it is night. Time in this city has made that warning sail old and worn and tattered, so that when the wind is cold and strong, holes you could put your fist though appear, and the wind can go through them, and delay the motion and the speed of arrival. But I was going nowhere in particular. I had no hour or appointment; and with this snow, I was just a man, an ordinary man, with no distinguishing markings or name, walking with no purpose other than a ritual walk to defeat the restricting snow and cold, at a time in my life when I should have been elsewhere dressed in too-long short pants named after an island I have never visited, with white soft shoes polished even whiter than the belt we put round our waists on parades in the hot sun when it is the Queen's Birthday, or when someone is passing out; or like the corked blancoed helmets of the Governor, when there were governors and pageantry and fun and parades and colonialism.

Each January, the snow becomes thicker and more difficult to negotiate, and seems to stick to my body like old white paint, except it has more weight; and I move just like that fishing boat we used to watch far out in the waves that behaved like it was sliding between hills and valleys. John and I spent hours on the sand the colour of an old, empty conch shell, looking at those waves, thinking where they went to when they left our eyesight, thinking how many ships had passed over them, thinking which wave bore a woman we would truly love and which ship would carry us from our governors and pageantry and fun and parades and colonialism. Of course, we did not live through anything like colonialism. It was just our fury and our imitating the words of men older and wiser that made us see ourselves sitting on that sand on that beach staring at waves that washed assertive and sullen strangers ashore who then lolled about our narrow streets as if they were born there; as if they were born there to rule there. We knew only the meaning of sitting on the sand, and wondering, and pretending we were that little boy in the poem we learned by heart in elementary school, the little boy who stood in his shoes and wondered, and wondered why? We did not wear shoes while we wondered whether the wave that licked our soles, the wave that brought the fateful cobbler into John's pink heel, that washed my uncle in, was the same wave born in another country, that had travelled alongside the steamer and the lady boat and deposited the little blackened piece of wood, or stick at our feet. In elementary school, the teacher stood one afternoon, with sweat pouring off his face as the tears poured from our eyes, and pounded sense into our heads and ears and backs and backsides because we had not remembered that a little piece of blackened stick, or wood, was properly known as "flotsam." We were acquainted with another "flotsam," since one or two of us, not John or I, were sometimes call the "flotsam of society." We thought of ourselves as that little boy in the poem about boys in shoes, standing and wondering.

It was about, it was, I think, a little before four on this cold day in January. And I was walking north along Yonge Street, in a kind of white valley, for the thickness of the snow had hidden the bright colours of the store windows from me, and I was alone. I could see only a shape or two ahead of me. And when I raised my head against the flakes that were blinding me, there was no sky, but only a channel of white though I knew I was travelling north because I had set out from the bottom of the street, by the lake, and if I was not travelling north, I would have been, by now, by this word or sentence, drowned.

I have thought, sometimes, at this age, with leisure, of attempting precisely that. Jumping into the lake. And on that afternoon of sun and light and sky, blue as the desire for a young school girl (John and I liked the same bright, hair-plaited girl), when we were sitting with cobblers in John's heel, and had not seen the tube float out into deeper water, and could not retrieve the black, patched tube we had got from the Humber Hawk car which roared no more along the streets, once killing not only chickens but a man who had moved too slowly. When we looked up to see the tube, a million times larger than the lifesavers we were sucking, I was rendered unmovable as the Humber Hawk. I could not retrieve our lifesaver. Because I could not swim. And I know now, though I was too young to possess this heavy knowledge on that beach, that only those who can swim attempt to jump into the lake, to put an end to their lives. Those of us who cannot swim are too afraid of the water. We are like cats.

So, when I ducked my head and closed my eyes against the snow, I almost got knocked down by the person coming at me. He did not see me. I doubt that he noticed me. I was just another obstacle he had to walk around, or walk into, as he continued on in spirited childlike glee at the first snowfall that had transformed the sidewalk into a skating rink.

In all the fifty years I have lived in this city, I've never once tried to skate on ice, or rollers, and I never watch hockey games. The game that identifies me, through culture and the thick damp soil, is now forgotten, like other customs of that land from which I am torn. Cricket, to me, is now merely a figure of speech.

The snow through which I was trying to move, and in which I live, was a curtain, like the thick white ones my mother had set in each of the sixteen windows in our walled-house, with its six roofs or gables, six big waves against the wind and the blue sea, if you were sitting on the sand and watching it. And I could hardly see. I tried to imitate the sprightly form in front of me, moving faster to hide my fear of ice and thick snow, to make me less conspicuous in this white-coloured world, and hide from the person before me the fact that I was not born into this miserableness. And a new life came into my steps. My feet became less heavy. I was back there. And the wet khaki cut-down pants had dried suddenly in the sun and I was a sprinter running through thick green fields and this thick snow, when out of the blinding morning came a voice I had once heard many years ago. It was like a voice crying out from amongst thick white smoke belching from a burning house.

"What the arse you trying to do? Lick me down?"

I stopped moving. I could not stand motionless for the snow was underpinned with ice. My shoes were sliding; and I went back to that time, on a pasture so hot and so sticking wet, when I was made to stand at attention while the Governor moved through our files and I could barely see him in the distance, he being nothing more than a bunch of feathers all white, as if he were a gigantic fowl-cock about to crow the morning in, and bring his hundred hens to sexual attention. The voice, though, was a voice I had heard next to me as I wavered while ordered to stand "at attenshun!" – when the water in my bladder was making it impossible to be rigid, when I moved ever so slightly to ease the pain and the burning of the sun and the sweat pouring down my face into the white blancoed belt we had changed from green canvas to spotless white.

I was now close enough to see. And to wonder. And to call back, in this thickening morning, all those years in this flash of time.

"John?"

"Jesus Christ!" he said. I was sitting beside him on the sand, and the waves were washing in slowly, and the black piercing, punishing cobblers were in his pink heel. And the tube was drifting out, into the sea, into the ocean, into the Atlantic which we knew would join us after having separated us, in a land too far for our young eyes to see.

"Jesus Christ!" I said, giving the miracle credence and reality, giving the greeting its incredulity, giving the meeting its impor-tance.

"Tom?" he asked, believing and not believing.

How could he believe easily, in the mist of time, in this street, in this city, in this country which we had only studied in our geography books at Combermere, but had refused to think of seriously as a place where we would voluntarily suffer; suffer its cold and its ice and its snow.

"I don't believe my fucking eyes!"

"Man, this is too good to be true!"

"Jesus Christ!"

"Be-Christ, if anybody had tell me that you and me last see each other that afternoon we was sitting down 'pon the beach! Be-Jesus-Christ, look at this thing, though! God bless my eyesight! How long you here?"

"This is really you?"

"Is me, man!"

"Be-Jesus-Christ! Not calling the name of the Lord in vain, but this is a fucking…. But tell me, though! Tell me something. I been thinking of this for donkey-years. You learn to swim yet?"

And our laughter exploded, and from the white mist came bodies which paused to look, to scorn, to wonder what this joy was and what could cause such joy, that these two old black men would be embracing and laughing and pummelling each other on their thick black cashmere winter coats, with hands magnified in brown leather gloves, weighing down our hands and making us walk, after all these years in this new cold environment, like monkeys because we have never got accustomed to, nor learned how to walk, in winter.

We were hugging each other; I slapping him; he slapping me on the back, as if he was trying to make me burp, as our mothers did after the bottle; and changing from the left shoulder to the right, when that first shoulder blade had suffered enough pummelling from the affection that was born on that sand the colour of coral, and the empty conch shell.

"I don't believe my fucking eyes!"

"If you want to know," I said, "if you want to know the truth, I was thinking that very thing before I bounce into you."

"Bounce into me? Man, you nearly licked me to fuck down. And a black man like me don't look too good sprawl-out on the snow. I never learned to walk in winter. Been in England for years. Tried Europe for a piece. France and Italy. Got fed up with their brand o' racism. Liberté, equalité could kiss my arse! And I never learn to speak a goddamn vowel, in any of their fucking foreign tongues, neither! Stayed pure fucking Bajan! But you was about to say something when I interrupt you. What was you saying when I butt-in?"

"I still can't swim!"

He hollered so much, so loudly and so warmly, that I could see the cheap candles in the window of the store we were standing in front of, and I could see shoes with shiny leather and stiff lasts, and the shirts made famous in movies about men who could chop down trees tall as skyscrapers; I could see the sidewalk, and to my right, I could see the long windows of glass with shirts made in foreign countries by foreign hands, Polo, Yves Saint Laurent; and briefcases and travel bags from the sides of animals killed illegally. I could see where I was standing and where we were going. It was as if his breath, and the violence he had put into his laughter, was an exuberance of warmth. The snow had disappeared, it seemed, and around us the street and the sidewalk had come alive, but also I was sure that we two old black men, as they called us in this city, two old West Indian men from the old school, from the old conch days, were the only two living persons in the world. It was like sitting on that sand, possessing the entire beach, conquerors of the entire beach with no one in sight, no one a pretender to our throne.

"Where is the nearest bar? This calls for a drink!"

"Not drink, man! Drinks!"

"Do you have work to go back to?"

"Man, I am free! Work is for new immigrants, or stupid people. Work? Man, I stop working ten years now? I decide not to lift another fucking straw in this country, since 1980-something. November the 22nd nineteen hundred and eight-one to be exact. I have it written down in my wallet. Right here. When we sit down, I going show you the note I write to myself, November the 22nd nineteen eight-one."

The bar was almost empty. We moved to the back, in the semi-darkness, away from the entrance, to give rein and space to the explosion of our happiness.

"I can't ask if you drink the same, since when we last was together, neither you nor me was drinking. To me, you look like o scotch man. Right?"

"Scotch and soda."

"Jesus Christ! Something I was watching on television lately about twins, and their habits. Generic twins. Where one goes, even secretly, the other is sure to go. Who one foops, the other one is sure to foop. Now, how the arse would I know, your drink is scotch, after all this time? Thirty years? Forty?"

"Fifty! Fifty years! 'Twas nineteen forty-three, and the War was still on. You were ten at the time. I was the same age."

"And you haven't learn to swim in all this time! Those cobblers that I stepped on! I didn't have the chance to tell you, seeing that you left soon after, but the night when I went home, my mother warmed some candle-grease and made it into a poultice, and you shoulda seen how those blasted cobblers came outta my heel. At least one inch long, the average. And when I was living in France, one afternoon as I taking a stroll along the Elysses, or whatever you call it, all of a sudden I see this stall full of those blasted cobblers. I stand up. *Mon Dieu!* I was walking with my French wife, Jesus Christ! Imagine seeing cobblers in France! I tried to explain to her why I won't let a cobbler pass my lips. The French eat cobblers. The French eat anything, if you ask me. They call it *hot cuisine.* In the five years I live at home after you went away, a sea egg never passed my lips. Far less a cobbler. In the six years I was *parley-vous* to that woman, my wife, she never spoke a word o' English. And I never *parlaid-vous.* But we had two children. And that shows you that somehow we manage to communicate."

I was laughing as he said this. And I wanted to hear more about his life in France. I had never been to France, even though it was a short trip from London where I spent one summer day a few years ago, and froze. But he was reading my mind. And he went on, speaking with the same broad, flat Barbadian accent, although I imagined a touch of a French accent to his speech, thin and delicate as pastry.

He was wearing a tailored suit. Dark and with a pin stripe. His shirt was custom-made and white, with French cuffs. The cufflinks were conservative, thin ovals of gold. His tie was dark grey and shiny, and silk, and tied in a knot that was tight and elongated. There was stiffness in the neck of his collar and his cuffs. I could not see his shoes. The room was too dim, and he held them under the round black shiny table. But I imagined they were black leather. He was always fastidious in dress. And I remembered seeing him standing at the bus stop on mornings at eight, stiff in his khaki uniform pants, the white shirt his mother had starched and ironed with the flat clothes iron; and some Saturday afternoons, I sat on his verandah when no breeze could cool the hotness of the day, and I heard the frightening hiss of the iron as his mother touched it with the damp cloth to test its heat, singing as she moved the iron over the sea-island cotton shirt, *The Day Thou Gavest.* Her voice was good enough for her to be in a choral group. And it was her love of singing which he had inherited, and which had infected me, and which urged us to join the choir of the St. Michael's Cathedral, choirboys in bright red soutanes. He loved his soutane. He was a lover of clothes. And was responsible for me dropping my "slovenly shabbiness." He was always using big words, words bigger than our natural vocabulary. But he read four library books a week. So, watching him now, as he talked with the same school yard colloquialness, it struck me that he was using it to take us back to that day sitting on the sand, ignoring the intervening years, not wanting to bring attention or significance to the time that had slipped past.

We were on our second scotch. He had ordered Chivas Regal, "The best," he said.

"Over-rated," I said.

"Is said to be the best. It's therefore the best. Can't beat advertising. It's *supposed* to be the best of scotches."

"Teachers, for me."

"You still feel I'm too conspicuous. Remember my English accent? And I was going to England to polish it up. Well, I went to Oxford, as I said I was going. Where did you go?"

"Trinity."

"Dublin? Now you say it, I think I remember the girl we was both in love with, Cynthia. Met her in France one summer, she tell me she heard you was studying English at Trinity College, Dublin."

"Trinity College, Toronto."

"Well, Jesus Christ, man! If it ain't Dublin, you just can't tell a man Trinity! So, you still didn't learn to swim?"

"This scotch ain't doing anything for me. Martinis?"

It was evening outside. The lights in the bar were now visible, although they had been burning the whole time; but the colour of the light through the fake Tiffany lamps became a magic lantern leading us back to those dying afternoons when gold and God, man and the seawater, blue and a streak of silver, held us in its power, in its thrall.

"Children?"

"Ten."

"From the mademoiselle?" I was teasing. He smiled, and gold showed discreetly at the right side of his mouth. All his original teeth were still in his mouth, the gold was a filling. Men from our village who went to Curaçao and to Aruba to help find and refine oil, returned to Barbados, after two years, and three years, and five years, with their pockets loaded with guilders and their mouths gilded in gold, speaking a version of American twang, although the national language was either broken English or Dutch. Seeing the flash of gold in John's mouth reminded me of my uncle on my father's side who had come back with new suits made in Holland, hundreds of guilders in cash in his pockets, pink silk shirts, a colour we reserved for women, calling us, 'ombre, his retention of the Spanish word, and calling those who had remained, "niggers." We prayed that the oil-refining scheme would take him back to the rough barracks of Aruba, which he said housed only 'ombres. But John was speaking while my mind wandered. My mind wanders very often these days, and so too when I was younger. They say that professors are absent-minded. Well, I was a professor from the age of twenty-seven, and my mind was wandering then. Now, my memory wanders. And this early evening, for we have been here for several hours at least, I indulged my other habit. Dozing off. While reading. While drinking. Eating. And once a woman, who shall in the circumstances, remain nameless, accused me to my face, that I had dozed off while making love. I was too embarrassed to ask her if she had heard this from one of her friends, or if I had been in the unhappy thighs of a censuring love, when I dozed off. If decorum and propriety had not buckled me, I would have told her that it was my peaceful appreciation of her love that caused me to savor its passion and recover from its exhaustion by taking that nose-dive of a doze.

But John had been talking while I was wandering, giving me his history, which after all is what the drinking was for.

"Paris was cold, and I spoke no French, she didn't learn Barbadian. We went home twice on holiday though. She spend her time at the Alliance Fransays, and I in the rum shop around the corner from the beach where you and me used to sit and look at the sea. Ten children. But not from one woman. I have two from the *parley-vous* lady. Monique and Faye. Forty and thirty-nine. After I left France, I spent a time in Italy, I got married and had three of the prettiest bambinos. Roberto, Ricardo and Umberto. Thirty-three, thirty-two and thirty-one. A sociologist, a psychiatrist and an anthropologist. In that order. Professors at the University of Rome. I been making geniuses. Got fed up with Rome and Italian women, and seeing that I am an Anglican, the Pope was no help. Never picked up Italian in the ten years I was in Rome drinking scotch and eating spaghetti and watching Fellini movies. My wife, God bless her soul, was fluent in English and French. Then it was to the deep South. The South is the best place for an *'ombre* like me to live. Was practising in a firm of corporation lawyers. Made more money, but got lonely as hell. Those southern nights. And the smell. Patchouli and magnolia. Jesus Christ, pardner, and the food! Have you seen American mommas, and wonder why they are so goddamn *big*? It remind me of Barbados, though I never go back to the West Indies, and be-Christ, barring the time I took the *parley-vous* lady there to meet my mother, who was dying, I tell you, goddamn, next time you see or hear that I gone back to the West Indies, it is in a goddamn box, six foot long. But never mind that! In the South, the mommas remind me of that calypso by Lord Kitchener. *Sugar bum-bum.* Listen to me. Man, listen to me, man! When they walk, and they start to shake, and you see all that goddamn sweetness. Goddamn!"

He shook his head the way we had seen Mohammed Ali shake his head when a hard punch from Fraser landed. He shook his to clear his senses, to extricate himself from reminiscences.

"Goddamn!" he said, and I found it easy to picture him deep in Alabama, Mississippi, South Carolina or Georgia. And I could do this because in all the time we had been drinking, he had talked in his native, broad, flat Barbadian accent, remembering the taste of that life. "Goddamn! You hear of lil men liking big women? You heard them stories of these lil men coming on strong, and these big goddamn American women sitting down on them. I mean *sitting* on them. A man be one hundred and fifty pounds, goddamn. And this American momma be two hundred and seventy pounds, naked, jack! Goddamn! Well, it ain't no goddamn fairy tale. It be the goddamn truth!"

I was laughing so loudly that some women fresh from work looked in our direction, stared, did something with their mouths, and spoke. I heard the word, "Americans!" But I knew the term stood for something else, unmentionable, spoken with flat venom, distaste, utter disapproval. I had thought, for years, certainly in the last ten, to pull up stakes, put my bank balance in my pocket, and drive slowly down South, as I did not intend any longer to stomach the discreet disdain of so many Canadian women and men. But life in this city was easy, and good, and I had made money, discreetly on the side. From the stock market and from the race track, which is the same damn thing. They both have tote boards with shimmering computer lights and numerals. And men at both boards are always shouting, and cheating. I had made good; I was good; I'm good, as Canadians say, discreetly.

The waiter, smiling, as he had been listening all the time to our talk, was standing between us. The round shining table was cluttered. My cigarettes and his cigars were on it; and the ash from the two had overflowed the small square ashtray. And the more the waiter changed the ashtray, the quicker it seemed, we piled it high.

"Now, this is what I want done this time. If you don't mind," John was saying to the waiter. His speech had taken on a friendly slur. He was drunk. The waiter thought he was merry. "If you don't mind me saying so. I don't wish to tell you how to do your job. I been a waiter myself, and I'll be goddamn mad if some son-of-a-bitch comes in my bar and tell me how to do my job. But this time, this time, I want to ask you to do me a lil favour. A lil favour. When you make the next two double martinis, pass the vermouth bottle, *unopen,* over the glass mouth. Measure-off two drops, two drops of Chivas in each glass, and after you pour-off the ice, fill-er-up, joe! Fill-er-up! I here talking to this son-of-a-bitch who I haven't rested my two goddamn eyes on, in forty…. No, fifty. Half-a-goddamn-century! Me and him born in Barbados. Been to the same school. This son-of-a-bitch came here. And I been travelling the world. We met on the street. A minute ago, I coming through the snow like a snow-removal, and this goodamn son-of-a-bitch, my ace-boon-coon, clogging up the white-people thoroughfare! Goddamn! Where you from?"

"Nova Scotia," the waiter said.

"Coulda sworn you had West Indian in you!"

"Grandmother."

"Goddamn! Pour yourself a drink, fella. Goddamn! Ain't this a bitch? We taking over North America, if y'all not careful." He glanced at the three women just off from work. They were chatting and giggling. As soon as he had said that, as soon as Buddy had agreed to follow his instructions about making the martinis, our third straight double, we forgot about the women and the snow outside and the winter that was still falling.

The pleasant shadows cast by the lamps, the odour of alcohol, of cigarettes and the pungency of cigars from Cuba, and the low unknown melodies being played by a machine we could not see, wrapped us in a comfort not so different from the warmth of the seawater we used to sit so close to, having the wind dry our bodies and our cut-down khaki pants.

"Children. I love my children. Won't forget them for hell. The mothers're something else again. I won't say they're all bitches, and I won't say they're all ladies. They did good things for me. They was goddamn good to me, when you come to think of it. And a man have to be goddamn honest in these things, at least once in his goddamn life. But my children. Which number was I at?"

"Two in France. And three in Italy."

"And I said I have ten. Every Christmas, wherever they are, goddamn, they gotta haul their arse and come wherever I am, with their mothers too. I insist on that. And we sit round this goddamn big table and eat like hogs. My children take after me. They boys and the girls. They can damn well eat. *That* they got from me. And once a year, the whole goddamn posse gets together in a place one o' the children decide, and we bring the grans, and have another goddamn ball. Is the only way to live. And I glad I am a man who could afford it. I say three in France, two in Italy?"

"Two in France. Three in Italy."

"You're goddamn right. And I said I have ten, no?"

"How'd you do it?"

"I was an only child like you. But I always say I want a big family. Didn't plan it with four women. And sure's hell didn't know all these goddamn wives would be non-West Indian. I'm sixty-six goddamn years. This year. August twenty-second. To be exact. I just been through my fourth divorce. Bitch took me for a loop. But she was kind. After the Italian opera singer."

"What did she sing?"

"She was Italian. Sure, she wasn't no goddamn opera singer. I calls her that. To *me*, she was a' opera singer. Now after *la-dolce-vita*, her name was Dolly, I try to make a life with a lady from Alabama, Wilhemina. Part German. Part Dutch. Part Austrian. Part French. And part Jewish. Life's just got to be parts, and more parts. Goddamn! Two hundred and seventy pounds of parts in her panties. A physicist. And love having children? Love having children? What a woman. I worships the ground that woman walk on."

"Where's she now?"

"Alabama. From her, I had four children. Every goddamn one turned out wrong. Bad. Terrible. The environment. Three boys and a girl. Age from twenty-eight to nineteen. Dope. Fast cars. Needles. Drinking. You think I been a bad influence? Tell me, man. Look me in the goddamn face, and tell me if, by having so many children, and four wives, I been a bad model for four goddamn delinquents that I gave birth to, with my wife?"

"And the tenth?"

He drank off the martini in two gulps. He beckoned Buddy over. He took out his cigar case, a huge crocodile case, and extracted a cigar. It said *Monte Cristo.* He took out his cigar clipper. He passed the match in a circular motion at the tip. He made short, almost silent puffs on the cigar. It was like the firing of a gun with a silencer attached to it. The tip glaring red. And he took a large draw, held the smoke, savoring its taste and its power as it went through his system. He closed his eyes for a moment. And when he opened them, the smoke shrouded my sight and then the cloud passed, and all that was left was the aroma of the expensive cigars. I wished I could smoke cigars.

"Don't ask," he said. "I'm not gonna tell you about this one, scion of my old age. Goddamn beautiful girl. Me and her mother aren't married. But I'm thinking of it. For goddamn sure. But I been yakking and yakking about me. You married?"

"No."

"Goddamn! You lucky son-of-a-bitch! How come no Canadian hauled your arse in a church in holy matrimony?"

"Too busy making money."

"You look good. Not a day upside of forty. And you dress well. One reason I'm here, to get me a good new cashmere top coat, in the same cut as yours. Stand up. No, stand up, lemme see how it hang. Good. That's the cut I'm looking for. Those tailors in America don't know one fuck about cut and drape and hang. So, you not married! Ever?"

"No, never."

"Doing well?"

"Can't complain."

"Car? House?"

"Benz in a garage round the corner. And a little place in Rosedale."

"What's Rosedale? A project? Community housing?"

"In a way, you could say so. But the joints in Rosedale cost half million to…."

"Goddamn! And me and you, sitting on a goddamn beach, in make-believe bathing trunks. Fifty goddamn years ago, and looking out into the goddamn sea! What did you see when you looked out in the sea? What did you see in the sea? What did you see?"

"Ships!"

"Ships," he said, and the way he said it, told me he was travelling back over all that time, perhaps not in a ship, but with the same movement. *"I saw three ships, come sailing in…."*

"Come sailing in, come sailing in," I continued.

And we laughed loudly, and two women in the now nearly empty room looked around and they looked unsober, and they laughed, and smiled with us.

"Ship sail," he said.

"Sail fast," I said.

"How many men on deck?" he said.

"Ten!" I said.

"That little girl I not been telling you about. That's why I'm here. I was just at the Sick Kids Hospital." He didn't say anymore. And I didn't ask.

The snow was still coming down and it seemed that a white sheet had been drawn against the window, preventing us from looking outside, from seeing the darkness. I thought of the mock battles we used to play in John's house, games sent to him by his father who spent all his life in America working on a ship, and when he came off, refused to come home. But he sent toys and pens and shoes which were brogues and heavy, and too large for John's feet, and shirts that lumberjacks wore. And none of these things John could take to school, or wear, for the headmaster said they were "Loud, and damn American."

"Children?" he asked me.

"No children."

"Are you a goddamn homosexual, then?"

"I don't think so," I said. And gave off a laugh. He was not relieved.

"You queer?" He was not smiling. The cigar was stuffed into his mouth, and his lips were tight around it, and smoke was coming out, it seemed, from his eyes even.

"I had a bad experience. She was Chinese. Very bright, and intelligent and lovely in a way. She was a law student from Shanghai."

"You been *Shanghaied!* You been took?"

"She was a translator before she was a law student. And she didn't study law in China but here at a small university. I met her five years ago when she was still a child, really. But she was beautiful and very bright, something like a computer mind and we used to walk to the Chinese market, and, this is what I was waiting for, after a few flings, and...."

"Chinese women're something else again, if you know what I mean! What's her name?"

"We had just bought the house in Rosedale, and she was in the last month of her law-thing, and was to be called to the Bar. We took a trip to China where we bought a lotta things, including rings. And she stayed behind and I was in the backyard in my garden, chasing squirrels from eating the goddamn tomatoes, when the telephone went. And I chased two more of those goddamn tree rats. The neighbour feeds them peanuts. So, I walk in the house through the French doors and took up my scotch on the way to the study, and sat down, and…."

"So!"

"I never got up from that chair for hours. Five years ago, on the ninth of July, to be exact. So, I walk this street out there, Yonge Street, as I used to leave the house which is just alongside the ravine, and walk up Yonge and meet her anywhere, on the way home. Five years every day, including Sundays. And sometimes, with the number of Chinese living now in this city, sometimes, I think I see her, and that the telephone message I got on the ninth of July five years ago, was just a joke, a prank someone played on me. But I was standing over her coffin, and I saw her in the coffin, I saw her face, and it was still beautiful, and her hair like a…."

"Don't," John said. "Buddy!" and Buddy came over. He removed the piled ashtrays, and said, "Same again?"

"No. Two brandies. Best in the house. You got some Spanish brandy?"

"Not another woman since. Not even an occasional woman, for company, or…."

"And all the time you're listening to me, shouting off my goddamn mouth!" he tapped his *Monte Cristo* on the edge of the cluttered ashtray, and looked me in the eye. "About the Sick Kids Hospital, that's where my daughter is. Intensive care."

Buddy brought the brandy. John lit a match and applied it to the glass. I drank mine off, in one gulp.

The snow had now completely isolated us from the sidewalk. There was no one else in the bar. Only Buddy polishing glasses, moving a bottle an inch, placing it an inch farther one way or the other, waves of bottles in the mirror. The music was not playing. And all we could hear was the passing of cars, the sound of slush and skids, and it sounded like the water that lapped our feet when we sat in the sun on the sand, beside the old conch shell the fishermen had used to summon villagers and to summon death.

"I didn't mean to suggest you was a homosexual, or anything."

"It never crossed my mind."

"We leave the cradle, man, and our mothers feed us Cream of Wheat to make us men and we have different paths, and we go here and we go there, have women, wives, girlfriends, but we never leave the place we're born. We never grow up, really. And it took me all the travel I been travelling to understand, we start out on a beach, two barefoot boys, looking out into the goddamn sea, and seeing things. Perhaps, we shouldn't have looked so hard. Perhaps, we should still be there on that beach, sitting on the sand, looking out at the ships and fishing boats."

"When Lee died, the first thing that came, the first thing that came into my mind, was that afternoon you and I were sitting on the beach. I sat at home in a chair, a grown man in my shoes, wondering, wondering why life would want to lick me down in Rosedale, and Rosedale, it's become *nothing*, nothing like that day on the beach, sitting on the sand beside you, and I ask myself why couldn't I see on that day, and at that time, that I'd meet this woman and have happiness for such a goddamn short space o' time? The loss is a long way to go for, a long way."

"Let's close this goddamn joint!"

"It is closed, man."

"Goddamn! And you still don't know how to swim!"

Questions for Discussion and Essays

Austin Clarke is the winner of the 2002 Giller Prize, the 2003 Commonwealth Writers Prize, and the 16th Annual Trillium Prize for *The Polished Hoe*, which was also long-listed for the 2004 International IMPAC Dublin Literary Award. He is the winner of the 1999 W.O. Mitchell Prize, awarded each year to a Canadian writer who has not only produced an outstanding body of work, but has been an outstanding mentor among young writers. He is the author of nine novels and six short story collection, including *Choosing His Coffin: The Best Stories of Austin Clarke, Growing Up Stupid Under the Union Jack, The Prime Minister*, and most recently, the culinary memoir, *Love and Sweet Food.*

1. What is the common theme of all the short stories?

2. How do you explain the meaning of the elevator, in "In an Elevator"?

3. Does the ride in the elevator upwards suggest the man's failure?

4. Do you think that "Ship Sail! Sail Fast!" portrays the corn growing beside the train tracks, as a suitable hiding place?

5. Would you say that the man on the train sees ghosts or real men and women, escaping?

6. In "The Cradle Will Fall," how does the author use dialogue to describe memoir?

7. What is the main point in "They're Not Coming Back"? The child's animosity towards her mother? Or the mother's neglect of her daughter?

8. In "If the Bough Breaks," what has happened to the white girl who comes into the salon?

9. What does the figure of Christophe contribute to "If the Bough Breaks"?

10. The title of this collection of short stories – *There Are No Elders* – is from a poem by a West Indian poet, the 1993 Nobel Laureate, Derek Walcott. The title of the Walcott poem, "The Saddhu of Couva," is from the book, *The Star-Apple Kingdom*. The following is a selection of the poem from which the title is extracted:

> *I talked too damn much on the Couva Village Council.*
> *I talked too softly. I was always drowned*
> *by the loudspeakers with the greatest pictures.*
> *I am best suited to stalk like a white cattle bird*
> *on legs of sticks, with sticking to the Path*
> *between the canes on a district road at dusk.*
> *Playing the Elder. There are no more elders.*
> *Is only old people.*

What do you think Clarke sees as the meaning of the title *There Are No Elders* for this book? How does it work for the book as a whole?

Related Reading

Algoo-Baksh, Stella. Austin C. Clarke: A Biography.
    Toronto: ECW Press, 1994.

Baldwin, James. *The Fire Next Time.*
    New York: Vintage, 1992.

Fanon, Frantz. *The Wretched of the Earth.* Translated by Richard
    Philcox.
    New York: Grove Press, 2005.

Fanon, Frantz. *Black Skin, White Masks.* Translated by Charles
    L. Markmann
    New York: Grove Press, 1967.

Lovelace, Earl. *Salt.*
    New York: Faber & Faber, 1996.

Whintrop, Jordan D. *White Over Black: American Attitudes toward
    the Negro, 1550 – 1812.*
    University of North Carolina Press. Institute of Early
    American History and Culture: Williamsburg Press, 1968.

Of Interest on the Web

1. www.pagitica.com/extras/austindialog.html
An interview with Austin Clarke at the Caffe Volo in downtown Toronto.

2. www.library.mcmaster.ca/archives/findaids/index.html
The McMaster University archives Web site. Direct Clarke link: library.mcmaster.ca/archives/findaids/fonds/c/clarke-a.htm

3. www.walrusmagazine.com/articles/2007.02.22-austin-clarke-interviews-malcolm-x
Austin Clarke interviews Malcolm X

Printed in August 2007
at Gauvin Press, Gatineau, Québec